Truth Tea
And
Other Stories

J.M.Clerkin

Copyright © 2024 by J.M. Clerkin
ISBN: 978-1-9161030-2-3 (Paperback)

For more information contact: jmclerkinstories@hotmail.com

For the tea drinkers of the world

TRUTH TEA

Tanya liked working as a receptionist in the Medical Clinic. She had been there now for close to a year. Before that, she had worked in the A & E. It was okay. People were usually nice, but the night shifts had been tough. Not only was she not a night owl but she didn't like the drunks and drugged the night brought in.

In the clinic, things were different. Sure, people could be grouchy but true trouble skipped their GP and went straight to A & E. Linda, the middle-aged divorcée who sat at Tanya's left-hand side, said that the clinic got its share of troublemakers, but so far the worst thing to happen wasn't a thing but a woman called Veronica who had a purple rinse and a tendency to lie. At least once a week, she arrived at the clinic without having made an appointment but claiming she had.

"She thinks," Linda had warned on Tanya's first day, "that if she just shows up here and lies about having an appointment, we'll just fit her in. Some neck on her. And before you go thinking she's got a touch of Alzheimer's or the like, I'll tell you now that woman is known to be a liar."

At first, Tanya didn't mind Veronica's made-up bookings. But pushing her in for a visit once per week was getting tedious, especially when there was nothing wrong with Veronica other than Fibber's Disease.

Veronica had just made her weekly visit to the clinic and taken her seat in the waiting room when Linda asked, "Have you been to that Saturday market in the church hall yet?"

Tanya didn't even know there was a church hall, never mind a market. "I haven't," she said. "Have you?"

"I have," Linda said. "There is some load of stuff there. Way more than I expected. I thought it would just be a bunch of old dears selling their knitwear and cake. But there are a couple of interesting stalls. One woman was even doing tarot cards."

"Yeah?" Tanya asked. She herself had never been

interested in them and was happy to just let the future play out.

Linda leaned towards Tanya. "There's a fella with an odd stall. Bits of everything he does be selling, and guess what he has?"

"Tarot cards?" Tanya asked. "Cake?"

"Truth tea," Linda said. "I was half-tempted to get some and test it out on Veronica inside. It would be some riot if it worked, wouldn't it?"

"Truth tea?" Tanya laughed. "Like tea, that if you drink it, would make you tell the truth?"

"That's what your man selling it was saying. He had me nearly convinced to try it but he didn't take card. He must've been about the only stall that was cash only."

"You don't actually think it would work though, do you?" Tanya asked.

Linda smiled, showing her two front teeth. The left front tooth had a chip in it after she'd fallen during the winter's freeze. "Truthfully, I don't know."

"Probably just some herbal stuff with a different label on the front," Tanya said.
She meant it when she said it. No tea could make you tell the truth. Even if by chance such a tea actually existed,

then it was unlikely to be found in a church hall in South Tipperary. If it did exist, Tanya would buy it, and she would use it. Oh, she would. Not on Veronica inside— that would be a waste. Tanya would use it on her fiancé, Garrett.

They had been together for three years. Met on Stephen's Night in the smoking area at O'Neil's. Had kissed within twenty minutes of being introduced. It was a fast love. Tanya had been worried that it would extinguish as quickly as it started. It wasn't until their first year together that she began to believe it had staying power. That belief had been strengthened on their second anniversary, when Garrett proposed in the same smoking area where they had met. All had been dandy for that next year. It was only after they hit the three-year mark that things started to go strange. Garrett, never the biggest talker, became almost wordless. If it wasn't for the little one-syllable answers, he'd have gotten the title of the Silent Man.

Tanya had asked Garrett repeatedly if he was feeling okay. "I'm grand," Garrett would say. He was always 'grand.' He got dressed each morning, put on a suit and tie, and headed off to show people around the houses that had zoomed up in price in the last two years. Then he'd come home and eat dinner. At least twice a week he would go to see his best friend, Gary, and the rest of the time he'd sit in front of the television, usually watching Netflix. His routine wasn't all that different from before. There were just a few differences. In the past, he had mixed video games somewhere into his routine and hit the gym three times a week. Those varieties were gone. As was their once healthy sex life.

Initially, Tanya thought he had slidden into depression. Well not slidden exactly. There was no sliding about it. It was a jump into depression. One day he was fine and the next he was a zombie. He had gone to Gary's stag do back in January. Had left the house that day as his usual upbeat self, and the next day when she saw him, he was the nearly silent man that he was now. Even at Gary's wedding in February, Garrett had been a shadow of himself. Sure, he was smiling and laughing, doing the part that everyone expected of him, but Tanya could see the emptiness behind his eyes.

"Are you doing anything nice for the weekend?" Linda had produced a donut from her handbag and was chewing a mouthful as she asked.

"Nothing exciting. Gym tomorrow morning, and coffee afterwards with the girls. That'll be about the extent of it."

"Check out that market on Saturday if you're staying around town. Other than the truth tea, there are quite a good few finds there. Nice selection of cake, too."

Tanya smiled. "You can't go wrong with a bit of cake."

"Have a little gander around," Linda said. "I'd go myself if I wasn't off away in Cork seeing my mother."

"Maybe I will go," Tanya said. She reached for her coffee cup and pressed the cold ceramic to her lips before realising it was empty. No point in filling it now, not when it was so near to finishing time. Twenty more minutes and they were free for the weekend.

At six o'clock, the clinic closed. Tanya took her green coat from the coat stand and put it on. She wished Linda a good weekend and left the practice.

It wasn't cold outside, but the sky was impossibly grey. Any minute it would open up and anyone standing under it would be drenched. Tanya picked up her speed and walked home. It wasn't far, only a five-minute walk, yet recently, she had started refusing Linda's offer to drive her home. Doing anything and everything she could to shift those final few pounds she had gained over the winter. As much as she didn't want to say it out loud, there was the fear that Garrett's new behaviour was because he just didn't fancy her anymore. That maybe his lack of interest in sex was because he had found someone who he did want to have sex with.

Tanya opened up the door to their house. As she closed it, the sky rumbled, and the rain began.

Garrett was in the kitchen. His dark blonde hair looked brown in the dark light. He was taking out a microwave meal as Tanya walked into the room.

"Hey," she said. "I just narrowly missed getting soaked to the skin."

"No way." He ripped off the plastic from the top of his meal. The rain plummeted against the window in the kitchen. Garrett glanced at it. "It's really coming down out there."

"It is," Tanya said. "You're not having a proper dinner tonight?"

"I am," Garrett said. "Bacon and cabbage."

"I thought we were going to cook?" Tanya asked.

Garrett shoved a forkful of potatoes into his mouth. His eyes rested on Tanya just for a beat before turning away. "I forgot."

"Oh," Tanya said. They hadn't cooked together in almost two months. Something that they used to do up until January. Not all new years brought in good starts. Not that Garrett's change had started on the first. It was the middle of the first month when it began.

"Tomorrow?" Garrett asked.

"Alright," Tanya said. She left him eating in the kitchen while she went upstairs and took a shower. When she came back a few minutes later, the plastic tray that had once held bacon and cabbage was cleaned out and put into the recycling, and Garrett was sitting in front of the television, his vacant eyes glued to the screen.

"You okay, Gar?" Tanya asked. She was standing in the doorway. Half of her body was slumped against the frame.

"Grand," he said.

"Nothing you want to tell me?" Tanya cleared her throat. "Anything at all?"

Garrett's eyes fell on Tanya again. A little flash in them. Pain? Disgust? There was definitely something

8

there. No time to decipher the meaning with Garrett's eyes back on the television. "It's still raining," he said.

It was; Tanya could hear it pounding down.

Tanya moved into the sitting room and sat on the edge of Garrett's armchair. "Do you want to go to the pub?"

Garrett switched off the television and got to his feet. "Actually, I'm going to meet Gary. But you go out. I'm sure one of your friends would go with you."

"Alright," Tanya said. She left the sitting room and went back into the kitchen. She was pretending to scroll on her phone when Garrett passed her. He wore his yellow raincoat. It always reminded Tanya of October and killer clowns.

"See you later," Garrett said.

"Bye," Tanya said.

She had no desire to message her friends to see if they wanted to go out. The phone was placed on the kitchen table, and there it remained for the rest of the night.

***

When Tanya woke up early the next morning, Garrett was asleep. She crept out of bed and went downstairs. It was early still.

The day stretched ahead of her. The sun was only

waking up. It would be a beautiful day today if the rays of sunlight stretching in through the slightly open curtain were anything to go by. Tanya opened the curtain completely and stared out at the little stretch of back garden. It was wet with the previous night's rain. Droplets of water fell from the washing line that Garrett had erected in the autumn.

Tanya loaded the washing machine and put it on the fast wash. No time to waste when the sun was expected to shine. She made herself tea and toast and sat at the kitchen table. She propped her phone against a vase and watched cat videos on YouTube while she ate her breakfast. Normally she would scroll on Facebook or Instagram in the morning, but seeing loved-up couples irritated her.

When the washing machine was finished, she put the clothes into the red basket and brought the clothes outside. It was only April but there was already a summer heat in the day. The weather report had gotten it right then. With a bit of luck, the clothes would be dry by the end of the day. Tanya hung her clothes on the line. The day Garrett installed it he had been giddy with laughter. She couldn't remember what he had been laughing about, but the ghost of the sound did laps around the garden. Garrett had loved to laugh. He was always laughing about something. Tanya thought she missed that sound just as much as she missed sex.

In the house, Garrett was standing in the kitchen, watching the kettle as it boiled.

"Morning," Tanya said.

"Morning." Garrett kept his eyes on the boiling kettle.

"You stayed out late last night." Tanya knew it had been later than he usually did because it had been after midnight when she went to sleep and there had been no sign of him.

"It wasn't that late." The kettle finished boiling, and Garrett poured the water onto the coffee granules in the mug.

"Have you much planned for today?" Tanya asked.

"No." Garrett looked at her. There was a yellow tinge to his eyes and red veins chiselled onto their surfaces. "You?"

"Going to the gym. Then I was going to check out that new Saturday market. You know the one in the church hall?"

Garrett shrugged. "Can't say I do." He turned around,

went to the fridge, and took out an unopened litre of milk.

"Would you like to go with me? It would be a good day to check it out. We could even go to O'Neil's afterwards for a drink?"

"I'm going to meet Gary at twelve." Garrett added a drop of milk to his tea and put the milk back into the fridge. "I'll be back later, though, to do the dinner thing. You have fun."

"Thanks," Tanya said.

She left him standing in the kitchen. His eyes vacant. His thoughts somewhere, anywhere, but definitely not on her.

After the gym, Tanya came back to the house and showered. No need to shower there when she lived so near. It had been a good workout, and her muscles ached. She wasn't going to go. She wanted to follow Garrett when he did leave. See if he did actually meet Gary and not the woman that she suspected he was seeing. Some of the signs were there: the lack of interest in sex and the emotional distance. But there were others that didn't make sense. Cheaters tended to take an interest in their appearance, but Garrett couldn't give a hoot and only wore tracksuit pants when he wasn't at work. Before, he had been a gym rat, but now his only exercise was the walks around the house.

Not like he was trying to impress himself, never mind anyone else. Maybe it was depression. Or Garrett was just plain old sick of the relationship. It was possible he had woken up in January and the whole getting married thing had repulsed him. Maybe being at his best friend's stag had woken him up to a future he no longer wanted. If that were so, then Tanya wished he'd just come clean and tell her. There was only so long she could live without truth.

Tanya pulled her jeans up. They were no longer tight. Her efforts over the last two months had made the scale and the inches go down. All that work to impress Garrett and he didn't even notice. Tanya's feet were heavy on the floor as she made her way over to the chair in the bedroom and pulled on her boots. She would have to talk to Garrett again. Sit him down and get him to confess once and for all what was going on. Plead with him, beg him for the truth.

"I'm grand," Tanya said. That's what he would say. That's all he ever said. "I'm grand." Tanya's voice was loud in the empty room. It was a girly room.

Unbelievably pink. Garrett hadn't chosen one item in there. He had left it all to her. Said he sold houses, but he couldn't care how they were decorated. At the time, Tanya had been delighted; now, she could only think of it as a sign that he had no intention of staying. The ring on her finger was only there for show. Tanya sighed. She knew that wasn't true. The relationship had been good. It really had.

Tanya's phone vibrated. She checked the message. One of her old school friends. Tanya had asked her if she fancied going to the church hall.

Can't today, hun. Going to Brian's parents. Have fun xx

Everyone was busy. All doing the couple thing. Tanya had been one of them only a few months before. How fast life changed.

She could text someone else. See if they fancied a stroll. But that would only lead to questions about where Garrett was. Before, they had been one of those annoying couples that were always together and now, they were mostly apart.

Tanya sighed as she stood up. Her legs were sore after the gym. She would just go to the market on her own.

She pulled the front door closed and put the key into her handbag. She stopped at the ATM outside Centra and took out a couple of twenties. The banknotes felt strange in her hand. Paper money was something she rarely used these days. Everything was card. Linda said most of the stalls took card but there were still a few that were cash only. Or was it just the stall that sold Truth Tea? Tanya couldn't remember. The conversation had only happened yesterday, but it felt like such a long time ago.

The soreness in Tanya's legs eased as she continued down the road. People were in good form in the warm weather. Tanya caught her reflection in the shiny glass of a bridal shop. Her short blonde hair was still wet from the shower, and her skin was flushed. Her North Face jacket, like the jeans, now fit her well. She mightn't have been as happy as everyone else around, but at least she looked healthy.

The church hall—Tanya had had to do a Google search—was located down one of the side streets. It belonged to the Church of Ireland. No wonder she hadn't known it when she could barely recognise the Catholic Church where she had made her communion and confirmation years before.

Both churches in the town had been built in the 1800s. Once a year, she attended the Catholic church for Christmas Day mass, and once in her life, she had been to the protestant church for a distant cousin's wedding. Tanya passed the latter church. She remembered the day of the wedding well. That had been when her parents still lived in Tipperary, in the bungalow where she had grown up and not in the villa in Spain. They had, after years of talking about it, left the sticks and bought their retirement home in the sun. The two of them were mad about Garrett and were always asking for them to visit. They did last year. It had been a good holiday, and Tanya had cried when it was time to go home. Not that she wanted to stay in Spain. She didn't. She was happy in Tipp. Liked the community, her friends, and the weather. Not to mention, Garrett was happy there, too. He was never going to move to Spain. Not even when they were old and retired and the cold froze their bones. That is, if they ever reached retirement age together. As much as Tanya didn't want to admit it, it was looking like something they might happen on separately.

Tanya walked in through the open gate. There was a

little silver caravan selling hot drinks outside the Church Hall. Tanya joined the queue. She recognised a few of the people in front of her but didn't know them enough to recall their names. The woman in front smiled.

"Beautiful day," the woman said.

Tanya agreed it was.

When the queue cleared, Tanya ordered a low-fat latte. She added sweetener and closed the lid. She sipped on it as she walked over to the Church Hall. Bunting stretched across the front of the building. Blue and gold—the Tipperary colours. No escaping pride of the county, no matter the church you attended. Although, really looking at the posters displayed in the small entrance hall, she realized it was more of a community hall than a space related to the church. You could attend a range of classes inside, from yoga to line dancing.

Tanya glanced at the posters and then went inside. It was busy. Not bustling but not quiet enough that inspecting the stalls would be awkward. And Tanya did inspect. She spent several minutes browsing organic beauty products before buying a bar of milk and cinnamon soap. And then she bought a flower-pressed bookmark. Not for herself, oh no; Tanya wasn't much of a reader, but her mother devoured books. It would make a nice item in the little hamper Tanya was making for her mother's birthday next month.

"How's the coffee?" a man, wearing a purple shirt and black trousers, asked. Tanya had been eyeing his stall up for a while. It was colourful and covered in a range of bits and bobs. There were clocks and ornaments and flowers and musical instruments, and a small section of food and drinks. Attached to the table was a sign that said: Jackser's Bazaar.

"Can you have a bazaar on a table?" Tanya asked.

"Course you can," the man said. "Sure, amn't I doing it?"

"You are, I suppose," Tanya said.

"No supposing about it," the man said. "And how is your coffee?"

Tanya felt the cup in her hand. The liquid inside was lukewarm now. "It's good."

"Pity you're not a tea drinker," the man said. He looked sadly at his little stack of teas. "I had such hopes that you were a tea drinker."

"You're the man who's selling the Truth Tea, aren't you?" Tanya asked. She felt a flutter of excitement in her stomach.

"I am indeed. My name is Jackser. Welcome to my bazaar." Jackser held out his hand. There was a collection of gold rings on his fingers. "And how, might I ask, did you know about my Truth Tea?"

"My friend, a woman I work with, was with you last week. Linda is her name. She said you were telling her about it. She wanted to buy some of it, only, you didn't take card."

Jackser smiled. "Cash only. As it was then and as it still is now. Cash is king, as the saying goes. But"— here he spoke in a lower voice— "I'll have to follow the leader and get myself one of them portable card readers." Jackser studied Tanya. His blue eyes were unblinking. "Here's a woman looking for the truth. Here's a woman who needs the truth."

Tanya laughed. Her cheeks were burning. She could feel the colour creeping onto them. Normally, they only reddened when she was after having a few. It was one of the first things Garrett had noticed about her on the night they had met. Only he thought she was wearing red blusher to match her dress. "I'd take a million euro."

Jackser was silent for a moment before saying, "A

million euro wouldn't give you the truth." He reached for a red box, so similar in shape and style to herbal tea. "But for ten euro, I'll sell you a box of Truth Tea. Let the tea brew for five minutes and then serve. When the cup is finished, you'll get your truth."

"Go way out of it," Tanya said. "Ten euro for a box of tea. And the box looks tiny."

"Not just tea," Jackser said. "This, my dear woman, is Ireland's finest Truth Tea. 30 bags in a box."

"You're joking," Tanya said. "No tea can tell you the truth."

"Oh, I love to joke, but I never joke about tea." Jackser put the red box back on top of the stack of boxes. There were two other red boxes on the stack, as well as a couple of yellows and purples. "But if you're not interested in the truth, then I have no business aiming to sell it to you."

Tanya laughed again. "You're claiming whoever drinks this tea will tell the truth."

"The truth and nothing but the truth," Jackser said.

Tanya eyed the box. There was a little cup on the front with steam swirling from the top. "Why is the box red? Looks more like love tea."

"Colour of fire," Jackser said, not missing a beat. "The

truth can burn."

Tanya nodded. "I suppose it can. Unless the truth is something good."

Jackser smiled. He tapped his fingers against the top of the box. "You ready to find out?"

A hundred more questions could be asked, but Tanya didn't feel like asking them. She had known she was going to buy the tea even before she had arrived. Had known as soon as she had set out that morning. Even if ten euros might seem a bit steep for a small box of tea, it was only the cost of two pints in the pub. Tanya took a tenner from her pocket and handed it over to Jackser. "I'm ready. I only hope it works."

Jackser gave the tea to Tanya. "Oh, it will work. Have no fear. The only thing you've left to fear is the truth itself. Make sure the truth is something you're really wanting to hear."

"It is," Tanya said. "It definitely is." The box felt warm in her hands. She put the tea into her handbag, and after she thanked Jackser, she left the hall and walked home.

Before going back to the house, Tanya popped into Supervalu and bought a cooked chicken, a bag of rooster potatoes, and a selection of vegetables. If they were really going to cook dinner tonight, it was best to keep it simple.

Garrett wasn't there when she arrived. His lack of presence was louder than the silence. Still, Tanya called his name. When there was no answer, Tanya went into the kitchen and set the food on the counter. Then she took the box of Truth Tea from her handbag and inspected it. *Truth Tea* was printed on the front, above the picture of the steaming mug. She turned it around and read the ingredients. 50% black tea. 50% truth leaves.

Tanya opened the box and looked inside. The teabags weren't packaged separately like in the herbal teas; they were loose and looked completely normal. "I must be mad," she said. "Mad or desperate." She debated making herself a mug but decided against it. The day was still warm. A perfect day to go outside with a glass of white. Not the right time for tea. Or maybe it was that she was a little nervous about testing the truth tea out on herself. Afraid of what lies she was keeping to herself.

Tanya poured herself a glass of white and went out to the garden. She sat on the wooden bench that could really use a clean and sipped on the wine. It tasted like the summer and good memories yet to be made. Tanya finished what was left in the bottle and when Garrett came home, she was heading towards tipsy town. She never reached the destination, though; the act of making and eating dinner had put a stop to her travelling.

Garrett's head was bowed in fierce concentration as he freed the potatoes from their skin. Tanya peeled and chopped the vegetables. When everything was cooking, Garrett scrolled through his phone. Tanya held her phone in her hand. She was still avoiding social media, but online shopping was a favourite pastime, even if she rarely bought anything. She wouldn't buy any new clothes until she was down another half a stone.

"How is Gary doing?" Tanya asked.

"Grand," Garrett said.

"I went off to the market in the Church Hall," Tanya said. Might as well be informative even if Garrett had no interest in asking.

"Was it good?" Garrett continued scrolling.

Tanya was glad she hadn't indulged in a cup of Truth Tea herself. If she had, this would have been the moment when the truth slipped free. "It was."

When dinner was ready, they sat at the table and ate it. Tanya tried making small talk for the first few minutes but then gave up. Without chatter, the only sound was the cutlery scratching against the plates.

They finished eating at the same time and looked at each other rather awkwardly.

"That was nice," Tanya said.

Garrett's eyes searched the room. They were always searching now. As if looking for a way out. "It was," he said.

"I'm going to stick the kettle on. Will you have a cup of tea?" Tanya was up and had her hand on the kettle before Garrett could reply.

"I will, sure," Garrett said.

The teas and coffees were kept in a press above the counter. Tanya had put the Truth Tea in amongst the herbals, knowing Garrett would never look in there. Even on the chance he did, he would just think it was a whimsical name for the tea. Sure, anyone would really. Tanya was pretty sure herself Truth Tea was just black tea with a cute name. Yet it didn't stop her from putting the teabag into the mug with a G for Garrett printed on the front. Tanya's mug had a T on its front. G and T. Gin and Tonic. Tanya had been drinking gin and tonic the night they had met. She always took that as a sign.

Tanya squeezed the teabag and removed it from her mug—just plain Barry's for her. Garrett liked his teabag in—all the better if it worked. If it worked. Tanya laughed at herself as she added milk to the mugs. This was insanity. She had reached it at twenty-seven. Love was meant to turn you crazy, though, wasn't it?

"What's so funny?" Garrett asked, his voice flat.

"Just thinking of something I heard a while back," Tanya said. She brought their tea over to the table and left their G and T mugs on little doilies that Linda had gifted her at Christmas. They were impossibly old-fashioned but also rather cute.

Garrett drank his tea. Tanya waited, expecting to see a grimace or hear a complaint, but nothing came. He just sat there, staring at the table and drinking.

"How's the tea?" Tanya asked. She could see he had already drunk three-quarters of it. Either it was that tasty or he was that eager to escape.

"Grand," Garrett said. "Yours?"

"Lovely." In truth, Tanya didn't think her tea was too great. There was too much milk and not enough sugar. "Garrett?" she asked.

He looked at her before gazing down at his tea.

"Tanya?"

"Do you like my hair blonde, or do you prefer it brown?" Tanya had asked him this many times before. The answer was either: "I like them both" or "they both look good."

"Honestly, Tan, I like it brown. I don't think the blonde suits you at all. And your hair looks wicked dry with all the bleach."

"Dry?" She touched her hair. Despite the reams of conditioner, it *was* dry, but she never thought Garrett had noticed. Especially in his current detached state.

"It is," Garrett said. "It feels like sandpaper." He drank what was left of his tea.

"Oh," Tanya said. A feather dropped into her stomach. She could feel the breeze it made on its way down. Either the tea, by some miracle, worked, or Garrett was becoming honest. "Did you like the dinner?"

"The chicken was bland, the potatoes were lumpy, and the vegetables were overcooked, but it was edible. Neither of us are great cooks, are we? We've put in hours trying to get better, and we're just not improving."

"That's not the reason why you've gone off doing the dinner with me though, is it?"

"No," Garrett said.

Tanya waited for him to give her more information. When none came, she knew she would have to probe. "What's the reason?"

Garrett looked at the corner of the room. He paled, and his eyes met Tanya's once again. "I feel like shite. Absolute shite."

"You're depressed?"

Garrett nodded. "At the least, you'd call it depression. More tormented."

"Did something happen?" Tanya tilted her body forwards.

"Yeah."

"What happened?" Tanya whispered.

"On Gary's stag do, I drove to Cahir. I was going to get a taxi home."

"I remember," Tanya said. She had been at Michelle's (Gary's other half) hen night and had spent the night sleeping on Michelle's sofa after a hard night on the gin.

"I drove home. I was well over the limit. Absolutely in the horrors. I…" Garrett glanced at the corner and closed his eyes. "I thought it was a tree stump or an animal at the most. If I had known, there's no way I would've kept driving."

"Oh my God." Tanya held her hand to her mouth. "You?"

"Yes," Garrett said. "I knocked someone down. An old man. He used to walk that road when he couldn't sleep. He was—, what do you call them? Insomniacs? He was one of them: an insomniac. He was never able to sleep. Anyone living in that area knew about him. They'd know to keep an eye out." Garrett laughed. "I know I shouldn't have been driving. I know it was awful. But the thing is, I went on the backroads to avoid cars—to avoid getting into an accident. I thought I was doing a good thing. You'd never think someone would be off strolling in the middle of the night on a boreen of a road."

"He…" Tanya stuttered. "He should've heard your car. He should've heard your car and stood to the side."

"His hearing was wicked bad, apparently. I suppose most people go like that by the time they're in their eighties. They gave him some write-up in the paper. He got half a page. His whole life story. I think it was to guilt the driver of the car to come forward. And I can tell you it almost worked. I've been battling every day trying to decide if I'll hand myself into the guards or not." Garrett stood up and walked over to the window. The laundry was still out since the morning, and it was blowing gently in the wind.

Tanya followed Garrett and placed a hand on his arm. "I know it was terrible. No doubt about it. You made a mistake. And drink driving is not something that you've ever done before, is it?"

"No," Garrett whispered. "I've always hated people who do it. I hate myself for doing it."

"It was an unfortunate mistake. But it would've been worse if it was someone young. Someone with their whole life ahead of them. And you said it yourself: you went out of the way to avoid getting into an accident. It's almost like it was meant to happen. Maybe the old fella would've gotten really sick. Maybe he would've had a death that lingered as it tore him apart."

"I still killed someone. I'm a monster."

"Your guilt is proof you're not a monster. Monsters don't beat themselves up the way you're doing." Tanya cupped Garrett's face in her shaking hands.

"Your hands are shaking," Garrett said. "You do think I'm a monster."

"No," Tanya said. "I...I'm relieved."

"Relieved?"

"I thought you were after…" Tanya ran her hands through her hair. It felt desert dry and thirsty. "I knew something was wrong with you. I thought you were depressed, cheating, or wanting to leave. Possibly all three. Knowing what's been wrong with you…knowing the only person between us is an old man is a relief. Assuming that's all that's been bothering you?"

"It is. I'd never…I'd never cheat on you." Garrett laughed. "How could you even think that? Sure, we have a great relationship."

"Since January it's been…" Tanya hesitated; she needed the right word. "It's been different."

"Since I killed an old man," Garrett said.

"Now I know it can be great again," Tanya said. "We'll work on the issues together."

Garrett sighed. "I really wish that were true, but it can't be great again. I might as well hand myself in today, Tan."

"Hand yourself in?" Tanya caught sight of her reflection in the window. Her eyes were wide, and her hair was sticking up at odd angles around her head. "You're a young man; you've still got your life ahead of you. That man…"

"Michael Finnerty," Garrett said. There was nothing of interest in the corner of the room—it was just an undecorated point where the two walls met—but Garrett's attention was focused there. "Michael bloody Finnerty. If only he had stayed inside. If only I hadn't been such a gobshite and waited for a taxi to get home. Too many if onlys and nothing I can do about it. I can't get my old life back. He won't let me."

"You have to let you. It was an accident. Learn the lesson and move on. You can't kill two people just because you made a mistake. Three people, actually: when you go to jail, my life will be over, too. Everything that we had planned will die, too. All the dreams. All the hopes. Everything will be dead."

Garrett broke his trance to look at Tanya. "I can't go on like this, Tan. I have to go to the guards."

"Listen to me." Tanya held onto Garrett's face once again. "You can't do that. It would be madness. I'm the only one who knows what you did, amn't I?"

Garrett gave a little nod of the head.

"I'll never tell on you. I'm your judge and jury, and I'm telling you to let this go. No one else will ever know.

31

If you haven't been caught, then you'll never be. And sure, isn't there always the chance it wasn't you? You said you thought it was a stick or, at worst, an animal. Maybe that's all it was. It could've been someone else who ran down the auld fella."

"There was blood on the bonnet. I saw it the next day. Not a whole lot, but it was still there. No denying it was me. It was."

"The blood could've been from…" Tanya frowned. "It could've been an animal. Some fox or something. Sure, you'd always see their bodies on the side of the road."

Garrett shook his head. His eyes scanned the room until they focused on the fridge.

"Are you hungry or something?" Tanya asked. "You might need something sweet. I could use something sweet myself. The thought of you going to jail is putting me into shock."

"I'm not hungry," Garrett said softly.

"Will I make you a cup of tea? Tea solves everything, doesn't it?"

"No. No tea for me."

"Why are you staring at the fridge?"

"I know I hit the man. I know it was definitely me that

killed him," Garrett's voice was still soft, almost a whisper.

"That's why you're staring at the fridge?"

"No. He's there. He's standing right in front of it."

Tanya didn't mean to laugh, but she did. "You're joking. Very funny, Garrett." Only, if the Truth Tea had worked, and Tanya highly suspected it had, then Garrett was indeed telling the truth.

"I'm not joking." Garrett had on his serious face. He had been wearing it since he started telling Tanya about the accident. "I wish I was. He's been following me since the day after the stag do. As soon as I saw the blood on the car, he appeared. He hasn't been following me for the fun of it, has he?"

Tanya followed Garrett's eyeline. "You're telling me you're looking at him right now?"

"I am," Garrett said.

Tanya bit her lip. "Describe to me what you're seeing."

Garrett took a deep breath. "Are you serious?"

"Yes."

"He's wearing grey trousers, a big, thick rain jacket, and rainboots. Is that what they're called? Rainboots?"

"Yes, or wellies," Tanya said.

They were silent for a few moments. Garrett turned his head and closed his eyes. Tanya watched him. There was anguish on his face. It was still there when he opened his eyes. "He just stands there and watches me. If he did something—if he smiled, if he frowned—that might be better, but just standing there and staring is driving me mad. And it's not just staring either. He looks right through me. Like he's trying to see what's inside of me."

"Does he speak?" Tanya asked.

"No. I wish he would. If he just told me what he wants." Garrett huffed. "Sure, I know what he wants. He wants me to go to the guards. He wants revenge for his death."

"Either that or he fancies you," Tanya said.

"It's not funny. If you were in my shoes, trust me, you wouldn't be cracking jokes. You'd understand why I've got to hand myself in. It's the only way to get rid of him."

"Garrett." Tanya took his hands in her own. "I bet he doesn't want you to go to the guards."

"You can't know that," Garrett said.

"Neither do you. And if that's not what he wants, then, not only have you ruined our lives, but you'll have him stuck with you in a tiny cell. If that's not a recipe for insanity, then I don't know what is."

"It has to be what he wants. It has to be. Unless it's just to torment me." Garrett rolled his knuckles along his skull. "I couldn't cope. I'm telling you, I couldn't cope if he just wanted to torment me."

Tanya placed her hands over Garrett's and brought them down to his sides. "Have you tried telling him that you're sorry?"

"No." Garrett looked shocked at the mention of an apology. "I haven't."

"Then tell him for goodness' sake. That might be all that he's looking for." Garrett stared at the fridge with unmoving eyes and a slightly parted mouth. Tanya squeezed his hands. "Just tell him, Garrett."

"I'm sorry, Michael." Garrett freed himself from Tanya's grasp and walked over to the fridge. "I had drink in me. I know it's no excuse. I know it shouldn't've happened. I didn't see you. I just didn't see you. And I didn't know what I had done. If I had known, I would've gotten help. That's no word of a lie. By the time I realised, it was the next day and by that stage, you were already dead."

Tanya walked up behind Garrett and put a hand on his shoulder. He turned around to her, his eyes were shining. She couldn't name the emotion she saw in them for a few minutes. It was only when Garrett said, "I think he's gone," that Tanya knew she had witnessed hope in Garrett's usually jaded eyes.

"Gone?" Tanya was smiling. Her future, the one that she had imagined for the last two years, was becoming a reality once again. "He's really gone?"

"I think so." Garrett beamed as he walked around the house. He checked every room and the garden before kissing Tanya. "There's no sign of him, Tan. This is the first time in months that he hasn't followed me." He kissed her again, this one with a little more passion flavouring it. "If only I had told you ages ago. Jesus, I would've been able to avoid the torment."

Tanya laughed. She had butterflies in her belly. She hadn't had them around Garrett since the early days of dating. "From now on, don't keep anything from me, alright?"

"I won't. And something else I'll never do is drive with drink in me. Never, ever again."

"Lesson learnt," Tanya said.

That Saturday night was the best one they had had since January. The best one since before that, too. It was like the early stage of dating, when everything was new and fresh. And the sex life that had vanished came back. All with the help of tea. As Tanya fell into sleep that night, she thought of the man Jackser and his bustling table at the market. She would pay him a visit. Thank him for the help his tea had brought. Maybe even bring him a gift—some wine, perhaps, or whiskey. He looked more like a whiskey man than a wine man. Then, there was sleep, and it was blissful and deep. Everything was alright and life was good.

***

On Sunday morning, the sun shone down on the laundry that was still out on the line. Tanya and Garrett got out of bed at lunchtime and slowly readied themselves for the day. Everything was wonderful. They even went for a drive to Cahir and walked through the woodland towards the Swiss Cottage. They had gone there on one of their earlier dates. Tanya couldn't remember which one exactly, but it had definitely been during the getting-to-know-you stage.

Throughout the day and especially on the walk, where

people or things could be hidden behind trees, Garrett was hypervigilant. Constantly watching and searching.

"He's gone, Gar," Tanya told him. "He's gone, and he's not coming back. All you needed was to apologise to him. Maybe there's a lesson in that: sometimes saying sorry is all that's needed."

"It's like being released from prison," Garrett said.

"Imagine how close you were to actually going to prison," Tanya said. "It would've been a nightmare."

Garrett shuddered before kissing Tanya on top of her head. "Thanks to you, that won't happen."

Tanya smiled. She might even buy Jackser a cake to go along with the whiskey. She'd get one of the cakes at Supervalu. They did the best cakes.

In the evening, they drove home. They had already eaten dinner in Cahir. No need to cook that night, and no need for Truth Tea. Tanya wasn't sure what she would do with the rest of the box. Maybe she would use it on the lying Veronica. That was always an option.

Just before going to bed that night, Tanya thought she saw something behind her. It was just a blur, really, but a man-shaped one. When she turned around, it was gone. Nothing there but the coat stand that they rarely used.

Sure, if anything was going to look like something, it would be the coat stand.

Tanya thought nothing of it. She went to bed and counted her blessings.

***

Linda was at work before Tanya on Monday morning. She sat in her seat, scrolling through her phone.

"Good morning, Linda." Tanya sat in her adjoining seat. "How was your weekend?"

"I'm after eating a house, and I can feel it in my stomach, but other than that, it was great." Linda broke free from her phone to inspect her co-worker. "Aren't you looking the bell of the ball? Someone's after having a good weekend."

"It was nice." Tanya smiled. "Peaceful."

Peaceful was the right word. She felt more rested than she had in months. Both mentally and physically. Her life was back. Her love was back.

"Peace is the way to go," Linda said. She made a slurping sound as she drank her coffee. Linda had a bag of croissants in the oversized handbag she kept underneath the desk. She held onto the top of the brown bag and opened it, holding it towards Tanya. "Would you like one? Only got them before coming here, so they'll be as fresh as anything."

"I'm alright. I had my breakfast already."

"Oh, I've had breakfast too," Linda said. "This is my second breakfast. I'm just like them hobbits." Linda laughed. "Sure, I'm short enough to be one."

At 8:30, the first patient of the day strolled into the practice. Mondays and Fridays were always their busiest days. It wasn't so bad on Friday, when you had the whole weekend in front of you, but having to deal with the busyness on a Monday with weekend brain was strenuous. That was at least how Tanya usually always felt. That day, she didn't mind. She beamed when the first patient walked in through the door.

"You're in great form today," Linda noted when the customer had left.

"Sure, where else would I want to be on a Monday morning rather than right here with you?" There were plenty of places that Tanya would rather be. Back home in bed with Garrett was first on the list.

"Well, I'd rather be in Spain. Drinking a Piña Colada and having sunscreen rubbed onto my back. Oh, it would be lovely, wouldn't it? If I could take five stone off before going, it would be even better. There you have it now: I've got my own life goals."

"Spain," Tanya said dreamingly. She would only love a trip to Spain herself. The beautiful weather of the last two days had melted away. It hadn't started raining, but the clouds were grey and threatening.

Tanya thought of a trip to Spain throughout the day. She was due days off work. A week away would be heavenly. It would be wonderful for Garrett, too. He always loved visiting her parents. Loved the cheap beer and food. She would broach the topic with him later during dinner. They had already arranged for Garrett to pick up ingredients for dinner, and since he finished work earlier that day than Tanya, he would start it. His talk of their disappointing cooking skills had been spoken about. They would both keep trying to get better. Maybe at some point, they could even do some cooking courses together.

"Good morning, ladies." Veronica was in front of the reception desk. She had had her hair done over the weekend and it was set in purple waves. "I'm here for my appointment."

"Your appointment?" Linda asked. "You haven't got an appointment."

"I have; the doctor said he'd put me down for Monday to come and see him. Said he'd mark it on his file and all."

Linda was about to argue when Tanya cut across. "Go ahead into the waiting area and you'll be seen. There's a good few ahead of you though."

Veronica smiled. There was lipstick on her yellowing teeth. "Thank you, ladies." Her pearls, the ones that she claimed were real but were actually bought half price in Penny's, clanked together as she walked away.

"I've had enough of her. There's not a hope she had an appointment. Shame I never got my hands on some of that tea." Linda laughed. "Jesus, imagine if it did work?" Linda didn't give Tanya a chance to reply before saying. "Too late now anyways. God only knows when he'll be back."

"Isn't the market a weekly thing?"

"The market is but the fella, Jackser, he was only stopping by for two weeks. He's like one of those old-school travelling salesmen."

Disappointment sank into Tanya's stomach. She had fully intended to go and see Jackser at the weekend with the bottle of whiskey. And maybe to see what other items he had on his table. Not that she needed anything. Not unless he sold cooking skills.

Veronica strolled past the desk an hour later. She waved at the women. "Hopefully I won't be seeing ye for a while. Have a good week, ladies."

"It'll be a great week if we don't see you," Linda said as she got up from her chair. Their workspace was separated from the front with a screened area and a door. Linda opened their door and went into the square hallway where the patients queued; from there, she walked to the front door and locked it, as was their custom at ten to one every lunchtime.

Tanya, for her part in their closing ritual, checked in the waiting room to see if there were any patients needing to be seen. Sometimes there were one or two, but mostly any patients still in the clinic were in with the doctors. On that day, there was one patient. He must have arrived when Tanya was making her cup of tea because she didn't recognise him. He stood in the middle of the room. His skin was leathery and covered in lines. And his faded brown eyes were hollow and staring. On his slim frame was a beige anorak, zipped and buttoned, and on his slim legs were grey pants.

"Heya," Tanya said. "What doctor is it you're waiting for?" Tanya only asked because one of the doctors, Martin O'Driscoll, would call once and only once. If the patient was in the bathroom, then he wouldn't call them again. It was, he seemed to think, up to the patient to knock on the door for their appointment. If the patient didn't know this, and it was lunch or closing time, then they would not be seen and would have to reschedule. Martin had been warned about his actions several times, but nothing was ever done about it. Doctors, even ones with bad manners, were too precious to dispose of.

When the man didn't speak but only continued staring, Tanya tried again. "Is it Dr. O'Driscoll or Dr. Musgraves?"

Nothing from the man. Only more staring.

"Sure, not to worry. I'll check the system, and we can find out." Tanya went back to the desk. Her computer's screensavers showed a picture of her and Garrett at a friend's wedding in the Maldives the previous year.

"Anyone left there?" Linda asked. She had produced a bar of chocolate from somewhere and was halfway through eating it.

"Just an old fella," Tanya said. "I'm just checking to

see who his doctor is. He's a bit on the quiet side. Won't tell me nothing." Tanya frowned at her computer. There were two patients who were booked in at quarter to one to see the doctors downstairs, and both of them were women. She told this to Linda.

"Must be someone's husband. Or someone's son," Linda said.

"His mother would have to be well into her hundreds," Tanya said. She knew the women in with the doctor and had seen them arrive. Neither woman was over sixty.

"I'll try and talk to him." Linda got off her seat and went into the waiting room. She came back shortly after. "No one's there," she said. "I even poked my head in the bathroom."

"Seriously?" Tanya asked.

"He's probably with one of them women," Linda said. She took another square of chocolate and nibbled on its side before throwing it into her mouth. "They must've just called him in."

The first woman, Ann, a redhead with too much perfume, came to the reception desk and paid her fee. A minute later, Gloria, a blonde with a permanent limp after a skiing accident, followed suit. Tanya thought he'd be with Gloria after it was clear he hadn't arrived with Ann. She even asked Gloria if she had an elderly man with her.

Gloria frowned. "I haven't."

Tanya searched through the clinic, starting downstairs and then upstairs. There wasn't a sign of him. The doctors upstairs had all gone on their break, but the ones downstairs were still in their rooms. Tanya asked them if they had seen the man, and neither of them had.

"I think," Linda said, putting on her coat, "he left. He probably came in when you were on your break, and I was chatting on my phone. Then, after you questioned him, he slipped out the fire exit."

Tanya chewed the inside of her lip. "But there's an alarm on the fire exit. We would've heard it going off."

"That alarm hasn't been on since Martin went back on the smokes again. He's been puffing away in that little alley, thinking no one knows what he's up to and then coming back in here reeking of smoke."

Tanya scratched her head. She had covered it in leave-in conditioner, but it just felt greasy and flaky now. "I guess you're right."

"Course I'm right," Linda said. "Now come on, and we get some food into our bellies before we die of starvation."

"Alright," Tanya said. They left the clinic. No one stayed there for lunch. If they didn't go home, they went to one of the nearby cafes. In the warmer weather, Tanya and Linda would grab a roll from Centra and sit on a bench in the park. That day, with the threat of rain ever present, they drove to Applegreen and ate their lunch there.

Tanya was tucking into her Subway when she saw the man again. He was standing in the middle of the shop, watching her. "Oh my God," Tanya said. There was a bit of lettuce sticking out of her mouth. She brushed it away. "He's over there."

"God?" Linda asked. "I could explain the disappearing old man, but if you're seeing God too, then I'd be starting to get worried."

"It's the old man," Tanya said. "He's standing over there by the bin."

Linda looked over at the bins. "The young fella in the tracksuit?"

"No, the—" The old man had gone from the bins. Standing nearby was a young man with ginger hair and sleep-deprived skin in a blue tracksuit. "He's gone. He was standing just there." Tanya scanned the building. There was no sign of him. "He was literally just there."

Linda laughed. "Looks like you've got yourself a stalker. No one ever stalks me. I wouldn't mind having one if they were good-looking. Wouldn't mind in the least." She took a bite of her burger and washed it down with Coke.

"Where the hell did he go?" Tanya said.

"He's probably just gone outside or went into the toilets," Linda said.

Tanya kept her eyes trained on the toilet, but the old man never came out. She managed a few more bites of her sub before leaving it down on the tray; all food would do now was turn her stomach.

At a quarter to two, they got into Linda's Fiesta and drove back to the clinic. Tanya was quiet on the drive, only adding little titbits to the conversation. Mostly, she kept her eyes trained on the world outside the window. It was a five-minute drive to Applegreen from the doctors' and took about twenty minutes to walk there. Tanya didn't doubt the old man could manage the walk, but she bet it would take him a lot longer than twenty minutes. Which meant it was likely he got a lift there. Still, she searched.

After lunch, the rush began and didn't stop. It was too busy for Tanya to think about the old man. Queues formed before her and Linda. There were those who needed a form stamped, a repeat prescription, or to see a doctor.

Nearing four o'clock, it eased. As soon as the slow-down came, Linda went to the loo. Tanya was currently ordering bloods for a young woman with long black hair.

"You'll get a text when the results are in," Tanya said.

The black-haired woman smiled and walked away. And then he was there, staring. Eyes piercing and burning.

Tanya jumped. She held her hand over her heart. "You knocked the life out of me. I mean, frightened. You frightened the life out of me."

Linda's chair creaked when she sat back down. "That feels much better now. I shouldn't have ordered the large."

"Oh my—" Tanya remembered Garrett's description of the old man's ghost. *He's wearing grey trousers, a big, thick rain jacket, and rain boots.* Tanya placed her hand on Linda's arm. "Can you see that?"

"That what?" Linda looked straight ahead. "What am I supposed to be looking for?"

"Can you see anyone there?" Tanya said. She felt cold. Incredibly cold. A fire of ice sizzled in her belly.

"See who's there?"

The old man walked closer to the reception desk. He smelled like decay. There was stubble on his chin and the faintest flecks of blood on his cheek. "Nothing," Tanya said. She closed her eyes, and when she opened them again, he was gone. "Just a shadow from outside."

Linda tilted her head. "You haven't been smoking anything, have you? Because if you have, I wouldn't mind some of it."

Tanya knew Linda was trying to be funny; she knew the older woman expected a smile in return for the joke, but she just couldn't manage to give her one. It was now past four. The clinic closed at six. Two more hours until home time. She could ask to go home, and Linda would oblige. Yet Garrett had never fled, and she wouldn't either.

"Would you like a cup of tea?" Tanya asked.

"I would indeed," Linda said. She handed over her

cup. There were droplets of coffee on the sides and a layer of brown at the bottom. Tanya brought it into the tiny canteen and rinsed out the cup as the kettle boiled. The light in the canteen flickered. A gust of cold air blew against Tanya's back. She turned around.

Slowly…slowly. The old man was there. Hollow eyes froze into her own.

"Please go away," Tanya said. "I didn't do anything to you." She closed her eyes again. The kettle came to a boil. Its steam mingled with the cold air in the room. "Please, leave me alone." Tanya's eyelids fluttered open. The old man had gone, but the room was still impossibly cold.

"Did you go to China for the tea?" Linda asked when Tanya sat back down.

"Sorry." Tanya drank from her tea. She had only dipped the teabag into the water and the resulting drink was far too weak.

Linda pulled her handbag towards her and retrieved a packet of shortbread. "Bicky?" she asked.

"I'm alright," Tanya said.

Tanya held her tea close to her chest. The coldness was no longer in the room, but it had seeped into her flesh and crawled all over her bones.

"Are you alright?" Linda asked.

Tanya took a drink of her tea. It was hot enough to scald. "I'm grand. Are you?"

"You're after getting wicked pale." Linda put the shortbread into her mouth and felt Tanya's forehead with a flat palm. "You're freezing, too."

"Probably just tired after the weekend. The Monday you'd be wrecked, wouldn't you?"

The GP's door nearest to the reception opened. Linda dropped her hand and gobbled the shortbread into her mouth. There had been a few complaints about Linda's untidiness and the constant sprinkles of food that she left behind. The doctor, a man with an unremarkable red face, strolled past. He nodded at the women and went up the stairs.

Tanya peered out behind the desk. There was no sign of the old man. He had left just his coldness again. She pondered taking out her phone and texting Garrett, but there was no point: in just over an hour, she would be back home and could talk to him in person.

Linda had her biscuit packet in hand again and pointed it towards Tanya. "You sure you won't have one?"

Tanya shook her head. Putting anything other than tea into her stomach would only make her throw up. For the next hour, a few patients trickled into the clinic. Tanya booked them in and did her best to act normal. As if that would terrify the old man away. Maybe, she thought, denying his existence would banish him to the otherworld. When he didn't show up for the next hour, she began to think that this was true. At ten to six, some of Tanya's nerves had abated and the hairs on her arms had settled back into their normal position. It was almost home time. All of the patients downstairs had been seen. Tanya had given the waiting area a tidy and sprayed it with the anti-bacterial spray; now it was just time to check upstairs.

Linda was laughing at something on her phone as Tanya passed. "You sure you don't want me to do the upstairs?" Linda asked.

"It's all good." Tanya had just taken a few steps up the stairs when the old man appeared. He stood in the middle of the stairs. Tanya gasped and took a step backwards.

He was staring. His face was ever unchanging. She wouldn't let him win. No way. Tanya closed her eyes and continued climbing the stairs. One step…two. He was right before her. Another step. And she walked into an ice realm made from nightmares.

No longer could she feel the stairs under her feet. Now there was uneven road underneath well-worn wellies. Water had slipped in through the wellies and one of the thin socks was soggy. At least the other one was still toasty. Tired eyes watched the night. They'd become accustomed to its darkness over the years and were able to see much more in the night than most. At least they could but time was slowly stealing the vision that had always been sharp. People used this as one of the reasons why he shouldn't be going out on the strolls. Never mind that at 86, he could still see better than most of them.

This wasn't just nighttime now though; this was the witching hour, when no mere mortal should be out. Never mind an old man with bad hearing. Yet another reason he was warned to stay inside. Easy to do the warning when they just didn't understand the loneliness that came when sleep didn't. It was better to walk and keep company with the night. Even the deep night, when shadows could look like ghosts. Ah, but the stars could be your friends. And there was always some animal about, as sleepless and restless as he. Or a human. Liz Quinn was an insomniac like himself. When she couldn't sleep, she paced in her front room or sat in her little glass porch, rocking in her chair and smoking cigar after cigar. None of the neighbours had words for Liz. Her insomnia didn't bother them when she stayed cushy inside.

Michael passed Liz's He could see the cigar's red cherry floating inside the porch. He waved at her, but he doubted she could see him. Hard to be adjusted to the night's light from inside a house. Not long after that, the car hit.

There was a flash of pain. And then there was the ground. Cold and wet from the rain. The car's tail lights were red stars going further and further away until the eyes that had seen so much over eight decades slid closed. Death was a demon shaking on the black tarmac. And the cold. Never had anything burned the bones like it.

Tanya stepped backwards. Linda was still cackling. The old man tilted his head just a fraction. Tanya edged her way downstairs. Her breath was sharp, and her heart was thumping. Ice-cold tears burned her cheeks as they fell.

Linda's eyes were soft and worried. She dropped her phone on her lap. "Are you okay?"

"I have to go home," Tanya said. "I think I'm going to vomit." Tanya grabbed her coat and handbag and ran to the door. She could hear Linda calling something after her.

The rain that had been threatening all day had finally fallen. Not just falling but bucketing down. Tanya thought of the washing she had hung under the hot sun. She had never taken it in. No longer sun-fresh but soaked with rain.

Tanya jostled her key into the lock and fell into the door. It was warm and snug inside, but it did little to help with the cold. The radio was playing in the kitchen. Garrett poked his head out of the door. He held a saucepan in one hand and a wooden spoon in the other. He was smiling until he saw the look on her face.

"I've seen him," Tanya said. "The old man—the ghost. He's coming to me now."

Garrett ordered her into the kitchen and made tea. Just the regular stuff for her. No need for Truth Tea when the truth was spilling from her mouth—so fast that she couldn't keep it from falling out.

"Jesus," Garrett said after she had told him everything.

"Did you ever walk into him?" Tanya asked. "Did you

ever feel his death?"

"No. I wouldn't have dared to walk through him." Garrett sighed. He ran a hand through his dark blonde hair. "I'll have to go to the Gardaí. There's no way I can have him stalking you now. You haven't done anything wrong."

"Go to the Gardaí?" Tanya's legs were shaking. She placed her hand down on her thigh and pushed the shakes into the tiled floor. Garrett had brought in the washing. It was in a basket by the patio doors. "You can't, Garrett. You just can't."

"It's what he wants. It's either that or you'll be followed by him for the rest of your life."

"He's left you alone because you apologised to him. You told him how sorry you are, so he's obviously looking for something from me too."

"Well, you can't apologise to him when you haven't done anything wrong." Garrett had been against the counter. He moved from it and took the seat next to Tanya.

"He must think I have," Tanya said. "Maybe it's because I know now and I'm keeping the secret."

Garrett took Tanya's cold hands in his own. "Which is

why I'm going to the guards. There's no other way."

Garrett had procured a blanket for Tanya as soon as she got in and it was wrapped around her shoulders. She was still freezing, though. She pulled it tighter. "We need to find out where he's buried. I'll go to the grave…*we'll* go to his grave. The two of us will. You've already said sorry to him and now I will, too. And I'll bring flowers or something. Maybe even one of them plastic candles you'd see in the graveyards."

Garrett frowned as he thought. "Is he here right now?"

Tanya didn't need to search the room to know he wasn't there. "No. He just pops up and leaves."

"It was like that for me too at the start. He gradually comes into your life, and then he doesn't leave. He used to watch me when I was sleeping."

"Is that why you couldn't…why we didn't do the deed for those months?"

Garrett nodded. "Hard to do anything when there's a dead old man watching you."

"I can't…I can't live my life like that," she whispered. She tightened her hold on Garrett's hands. "Tomorrow we'll go to his grave. The two of us, we'll take the day off from work. Can you take the day off?"

"I'll ring in sick."

"So will I," Tanya said. "After the way I rushed off today, I'd say Linda won't be expecting me in anyways."

"It mightn't work," Garrett said.

"I think it will," Tanya said. "If saying sorry worked for you, then going to the grave is an extra bit of grovelling and the flowers will be a cherry on top."

Garrett had looked so bright and full of life earlier, and now the hope had drained from his face, leaving purplish shadows under his eyes instead. "I hope so."

"It will," Tanya said. She was beginning to feel a little better. The idea that had come to her had been vapid, but now the more she thought about it, the more sense it made. The old man just wanted some recognition of what had happened. He wanted her to apologise for knowing and doing nothing about the secret.

The old man appeared two more times that night. Never when Garrett was there, though. The first time, Garrett was in the shower and Tanya was loading the damp clothes onto the clothes horse. Some of the chill had left her body in the hour since they had decided on visiting the grave—Garrett even knew where it was and had been debating visiting it since February—when she felt it creep back under her skin. She turned around and the old man was staring at her. Tanya heard the bathroom door open and Garrett move about in the bedroom. She ran from the kitchen, her feet angry on the floor. Not even the carpet on the stairs could soften the movement.

Tanya flung the bedroom door open, and the handle hit the plaster. In the two years they had lived in the house, they had never installed a door stopper. Both meaning to get around to it. They never did. Instead, they were gentle with the door to the point the movement was now muscle memory. The wall had never been damaged until that moment.

Garrett stood in front of the wardrobe. "You saw him again," he said. It wasn't a question. The likelihood of anything else putting that much fear into Tanya other than the old man was impossible.

Tanya sat in the chair in the corner of the room. "I did." She hugged her knees to her chest. "He must've been a right fucker when he was alive. A peeping fucking Tom."

"Everyone loved him. He was meant to be some fella."

"Maybe death changes people."

Tanya saw him once more that night. Just for a slip of time when Garrett was in the bathroom brushing his teeth. Tanya was already in bed, tucked under the covers, thinking that she was safe there. She was listening to Garrett move around in the bathroom when the old man appeared by the window. Tanya yelled, and Garrett ran in from the bathroom. In the few seconds it had taken him to get to the room, the spirit had vanished.

"How did you live like this for so long?" Tanya asked as Garrett slipped into bed.

"With agony. Pure agony. Tell you what, Tan, if this doesn't work tomorrow, then we're going to have to find someone who can banish ghosts. The ghost version of an exorcist."

Tanya pressed her head on Garrett's shoulder. His heart was roaring, and his skin was soft and warm. "This is what I want to hear you say," she said.

"Ghost talk turns you on?" Garrett asked.

"That you're determined to get rid of this bloody ghost and not content with throwing your life away." Tanya stared at the dimly lit ceiling. "But tomorrow will work. I've got a great feeling about this. A superb feeling."

***

The next morning, Tanya only saw the old man's ghost once. They had set the alarm for seven. Garrett had turned off the alarm and gone straight into the bathroom. Tanya, always a snoozer, was drifting back to sleep when she saw him. No time to even call Garrett before he appeared in the doorway.

"Not going back to sleep, are you, Tan?" Garrett asked.

"Not with a dead man watching over me."

After breakfast, they rang in sick. Or, in Tanya's case, she texted Linda and told her she had a stomach bug. Linda wasn't surprised in the least and wished her a speedy recovery.

It would mean an extra busy day for Linda but she would manage. For Garrett, it was a different story. In the years that Tanya had known Garrett, he had never once rung in sick. The prospect of losing a sale over a sore throat was far too much for him to bear and he had always pulled through the day regardless of how he was feeling.

That he had even taken the day off so they could visit the grave meant a lot to Tanya. She told him as much. "One day is nowhere as bad as missing years if I am sentenced to jail," Garrett said. "Plus, I get to spend the whole day with my favourite person. Let's just hope we aren't spotted going off."

Living in the centre of town had its benefits but it certainly didn't help for the times when staying hidden was necessary. Nevertheless, Tanya and Garrett went into the car, paying just a passing concern about being spotted. If someone did see them, it wasn't the end of the world. An excuse could be made. Really it didn't matter when fear of the living was minuscule compared to fear of the dead.

They left the town and drove to Cahir. Before going to the graveyard, the two popped into Aldi and bought a deluxe bouquet of flowers. The flowers were kept on Tanya's lap as Garrett drove to the graveyard. Their scent, especially the lilies, wafted upwards to Tanya's nose. "Do you like the smell of them?" Tanya asked. "The lilies?"

Garrett shrugged. "Most of them just smell the same to me."

"They're the flowers of death, did you know?"

"Yeah?" Garrett's eyes were focused on the road. His constant squinting was giving him premature crow's feet. Tanya suspected he needed glasses. She had said this to him once many moons ago, but he had shrugged the suggestion away. "That's interesting."

"May they help his ghost die," she whispered. Tanya looked out the window. It showed a blur of green. Rain that had held off since the previous night's downpour was beginning to spit again.

They arrived at the graveyard. Garrett parked his car on the road outside and they got out. Tanya held the flowers to her chest, as tender and possessive as a bride walking down the aisle with her bouquet. Although neither Tanya nor Garrett knew exactly where the old man was buried, the graveyard wasn't large enough to get lost in. They walked towards the newest additions in the cemetery.

Once on the short walk, despite Garrett standing next to her, Tanya thought she saw the old man. When she glanced behind her, it was just a man, grey and lined but still very much alive. His head was bowed, and his lips were moving as if he were saying a prayer. He was standing next to a woman. His mother perhaps. She had fluffy blonde hair and sharp eyes that met Tanya's. A cigar was in her mouth. She took a drag and exhaled grey smoke. Tanya left them to it and focused on the waterlogged path before her.

Michael Finnerty was buried in the middle of the graveyard's newcomers. His tombstone had yet to be erected. Instead, there was a wooden cross with his name engraved on a gold plaque.

"Here he is," Garrett said.

There was a stirring of grass on top of Michael's grave, but it would be months before it had any real substance. Next to the wooden cross were two planters with dying flowers inside. Only the ivy in the planters had any life left in them.

Tanya placed the bouquet on top of the growing grass. She was still crouched down when she turned to her fiancé. "Can you wait somewhere away? Where you're not looking?"

"You're hardly embarrassed talking to him with me here, are you? Sure, I did my sorry with you in the kitchen."

"He appears to me when you're not here. At least so far, he has."

Garrett nodded. "I'll wait in the car."

When Garrett was out of sight, the old man appeared at the head of the grave. "Michael," Tanya began. "I've brought you flowers." She pointed to them. There were drops of water on the plastic. Michael's ghost was unmoving and unflinching. "I just wanted to say how sorry I am Garrett accidentally killed you. He really didn't mean to do that. He's a good guy. He'd never drink and drive. But you know all of this. I know you do. You've forgiven him, haven't you?"

Michael's ghost kept on staring. His body rigid.

"I think you're following me now because…" Tanya turned her head away; there was a sharp pain between her eyes. "Because I know what Garrett did and I'm keeping the secret. But I love Garrett, I really do." Tanya flashed her engagement ring at Michael's ghost. "I couldn't tell on him. I wouldn't want him going to jail. Not for a mistake. Not for something he didn't even mean to do. And we've our whole lives ahead of us. We're hoping to get married in a year or so. If he went to jail over this, that couldn't happen. Between me and you, I couldn't marry a man who had gone to jail. I just couldn't." Tanya licked her lips. "Please forgive me. I'm keeping his secret only because I love him." Tanya closed her eyes, and when she opened them again, Michael's ghost wasn't there.

Tanya walked back to the car. The ever-present chill

had left her bones. She opened the passenger's door and got into the car.

Garrett was scrolling through his phone. He put the phone down and turned to Tanya. "How did it go?"

"He's gone," Tanya said.

"Yeah?" Garrett smiled. "Really gone?"

A Celtic Cross tombstone towered over the wall to the right-hand side. A lone crow stood on top of the cross, watching them. Its blue-black feathers were slick and shining in the morning sun. Tanya took Garrett's hand in her own. "Really, really gone."

They drove home and spent the rest of the day talking about their wedding. When they had grown tired of discussing wedding venues, Tanya went online and looked up dream wedding dresses. Life was good. Life was great.

For dinner, they ordered Chinese and opened the good bottle of white that had been in the fridge for too long. Garrett served the food on the fancy plates, usually only used for Christmas and Easter dinner. They even used the Waterford Crystal glasses for their wine. They were halfway through their food when the knock on the door came.

"Probably one of the neighbours. Maybe their electricity went off or something." Garrett left the room, leaving the kitchen door open just a smidgen.

Tanya went to close it. Not wanting anyone, neighbour or not, to see their fancy attempt at dinner. Things could easily get back to either of their workplaces. It wasn't a neighbour though. Two uniformed Gardaí stood outside. Tanya had seen them both around the town. One was in his twenties, while the other was in his fifties. Both were male with pasty skin and blue eyes.

"Are you Garrett Ryan with a car registration of 231-T-2078?"

"The one and only," Garrett said. "Don't tell me it's after being stolen?"

"Your car was identified as being at the scene of a hit-and-run that resulted in the death of Michael Finnerty…"

Sounds faded. Tanya's knees buckled. She steadied herself against the door. She heard a few other phrases. "Arresting you in relation to the death of Michael Finnerty."

Garrett left the house, but not before retrieving his coat from the coat stand and kissing Tanya on the cheek. She faded back to the kitchen and sat down and drank what was left of the wine.

It wasn't until months later that she would learn that Liz Quinn, Michael Finnerty's insomniac neighbour, had been the woman in the graveyard. Tanya had forgotten all about her after stepping out of the old man's ghost. Liz with eyes even sharper than Michael's, had recognised the car that struck her late neighbour. She had even managed to see the first few digits of the car reg before it was swallowed by the night.

Oh, Liz was a grand woman, but she was nosy. She always had been. She didn't know the two at the grave. Knew everyone else who visited it though. When she saw the black car they had come in, she had known exactly who they were. Liz got her hunches and followed them with her big nose in the air. From that night onwards, she slept through the night. A gift from Old Michael, she told people, now that he could rest easy with his death finally avenged.

.

LIAM OF THE RING

Sylvia left the warmth of her bed, stretched, and went into the living area. Sun shone in through the window. It hurt her hangover. The previous night, Sylvia and her neighbour, Jane, had been out at their local for drinks. Sylvia had spent the evening talking about the wedding she was going to the following weekend. Sylvia had agreed to go, thinking if she started taking dating seriously, then she wouldn't be single going to the wedding. She was in Dublin City and there were so many men out there. It would be no problem for her to meet someone. She had gone out on 26 dates now in close to six months and was bewildered to say her mission had failed. Despite knowing exactly what she wanted, she couldn't find it.

Sylvia made herself eggs and toast and poured herself a glass of water. She didn't drink breakfast tea or coffee. She didn't drink anything hot at all. The colder the drink, the better—true to the tune, Sylvia added frozen strawberries to her water.

There was a knock at the door to the sound of "Here Comes the Bride." Sylvia shook her head but nevertheless answered the door. Jane was standing there, dressed in her tracksuit, as black as basically everything else that she wore. Although Sylvia considered herself an outdoorsy person, she was nothing compared to Jane, who spent most of her free time running riot in the Dublin mountains.

"You just had to do it, didn't you?"

"I couldn't resist. Am I allowed in or…?"

"As long as you don't do that again."

They went into the kitchen. Jane had a wad of envelopes in her hand. She left them on the counter next to the glass of water. "Some of your letters were in my mailbox again. That new fella delivering them is some bleeding dope."

Sylvia took the cooling toast and put it on a large plate with the eggs. "And why were you only collecting your mail on a Sunday? I check every day after work." It was true, she did. There was never anything of interest there. She only ever received handwritten letters at Christmas. Anything else was a bill or a political leaflet. To receive a handwritten letter at any other time could only mean bad news.

"You alright?"

"I'm grand."

"You went all dozy there, staring off at the letters like they were revealing your future."

"Just lost in thought. You know what I'm like."

"Are you thinking about the wedding again?"

Sylvia buttered her toast. The butter was soft from the morning sun and it glided across the bread. "I'm thinking about eating my breakfast, if you must know."

"And then your annoying neighbour comes in and ruins your food," Jane said.

"I know." Sylvia brought the breakfast over to the counter and sat on a brown, leather stool.

"Done anymore thinking about if you're going to the wedding then?" Jane asked as she filled the kettle with water.

John, Sylvia's last boyfriend, had bought the kettle.

Before that, he used to boil the water for his tea in a saucepan.

"I might as well. I've paid for the bloody hotel room."

"And it's a weekend away. There's still every chance that you'll find the love of your life before then. Get swiping, and you never know."

Sylvia had swiped so much that her thumbs hurt. "Doubtful."

"You've made a list of the kind of partner you want to attract?" Jane had done it herself, and it had worked wonders for her. Now she was happily dating her partner, Leonie. Jane had spent an hour telling Sylvia all about the list the previous night.

"I'm only out of the bed twenty minutes ago. I haven't even had a moment to send a text message, never mind writing a list."

"Well, you can do it later then." Jane opened the cupboards and took out a mug. There were only three of them there—all presents over the last two Christmases from people who didn't know Sylvia enough to know that they'd be no use to her.

There had been reams of them when John lived in the apartment, but when things had ended between them,

Sylvia took his mugs and brought them to the charity shop. She often wondered where they fared. It was odd to imagine some stranger drinking from something that had belonged to John.

While Jane made her tea, Sylvia shuffled through the letters. All bills, as expected, and one reminder that her TV license was soon to expire. At the very end of the stack was a leaflet that advertised Dublin's Darling Market. "Think this is yours," Sylvia said, handing the leaflet to Jane.

Jane added milk to her tea. She saw the leaflet in Sylvia's hand. "It must've been in the mailbox. And I've got a sticker on the front saying not to be leaving me bleeding junk mail." Jane took the leaflet. "I would've gone to the bleeding thing and all."

"Why don't you go then?" Sylvia finished her first egg and slice of toast. "The mountains aren't going anywhere anytime soon."

Jane used a spoon to fish the teabag from the cup before dropping the bag into the sink.
She left the teaspoon on the counter and joined Sylvia on the opposite matching stool. "Nah, I hate cancelling plans. But you should go. You might meet the love of

your life there."

Sylvia raised her eyebrows. "You think that likely?"

"That you'll go to the market or meet the love of your life? I think both are possible." Jane left the leaflet next to Sylvia's plate. "Telling you, there could be a lot worse ways of spending your Sunday. Pity you won't join me and go to the mountains."

"I will next time, provided you're going on a Saturday."

"I'm going next Saturday," Jane said.

"And I'll be getting drunk with the rest of the spinsters. You know it's come to the point now where people don't even ask me if I'm seeing someone."

"I know. You kept telling me last night." Her mobile phone beeped. She read the message. "Leonie's waiting downstairs. I better make tracks." She took one final drink from her tea and left it half-finished in the sink. "And like I said last night, silence is better than them asking why you're single for the last two years. Now, are you sure that you don't want to come to the mountains?"

"I'm sure."

"When I see you again, tell me that you've at least made your list." Jane walked to the door. Sylvia followed and let her out.

"See you during the week."

"Oh, I'm sure you will." Sylvia waited until Jane had turned the corner before closing the door. Then she went back into the living space and finished her now cold breakfast. "Dublin's Darling Market." Sylvia ran her finger over the page. It had been a long time since she had visited a market.

In her childhood and early teens, she used to love them. They were hopeful places full of wonderful things. At a market, she envisioned herself finding a magical mirror that would allow her to contact her mother. She would discover that her mother had been stolen and was in another realm. Sylvia would bring her home and be a hero.

When Sylvia turned fifteen, she embraced the truth. Her mother had willingly left. Not without leaving a letter on the fireplace. Eleven-year-old Sylvia had come home from school and opened it. She had been excited out of her mind, thinking that someone had left her a present. Maybe even a late Christmas card from an unknown relative. Inside was a farewell and a request for her grandparents to be the new caregivers.

After Sylvia had stripped her bed and done the rest of the Sunday chores, it was not long after two. Sylvia took a glass of water out onto the balcony and sat on her little wicker chair. Her laundry was drying on a clothes rack next to the chair. It was beautiful out on the balcony, and it caught the sun for so much of the day. It was her own little retreat from the busy world.

On warm and sunny Sundays, she'd spend the whole of the day out here. But that day, she was restless. She wanted to be doing something. Sylvia went inside and put on her coat and boots. She gazed at her reflection in the hallway mirror. At 37, she didn't look that much different than she had in her early twenties.

There were no greys in her long, curly black hair, and her brown skin was unwrinkled, barring a few lines around the eyes. At the weekends, she still dressed how she had back then, too. Weekdays were for black and grey suits and serious shoes. At the weekend, she wore the colours she loved. They were there in the mirror: her bright red coat and her electric purple boots. Underneath the coat was a flowy, green dress that reached her knees.

Sylvia smiled at her reflection and then went back into

the kitchen, and took the pamphlet for the flea market, and put it into her handbag. She would pay it a visit. If there were any mirrors that connected to her mother, then she would smash them.

Sylvia walked alongside the canal to the market. It was on in the Blue Velvet, a venue that hosted a variety of events. Nearing Portobello, she took off her light summer coat and draped it across her arm. Much different weather than her last visit to the Blue Velvet, when the weather had been cold enough to burn. She had gone to see a Burlesque show with one of the many social groups that she had joined after John. It had been a good night until she saw a man there that reminded her of him. For the rest of the evening, her eyes sought out the man, needing to be sure that it wasn't John sitting with the pretty blonde.

Sylvia let the memory fade away. No point stewing on it now. She would choose to remember it as a good night. Most of the group events were a great laugh. Sylvia had stopped attending them when she agreed to go to the wedding and had begun spending much of her free time going on dates.

Most of the men she went on dates with were lovely.

Two of them she had met several times. Surely one of them would agree to go with her to the wedding. They'd get a free weekend away. She'd even hire out a suit if they needed one. Sylvia contemplated the idea as she walked to the venue, but she knew she couldn't do it: she had deleted all the numbers from her phone as soon as she realised it wasn't going anywhere. And unless one of them got into contact in the next day or two, then it would never happen. Pity she hadn't kept that as an option before getting delete-happy.

Sylvia sighed as she crossed the road. She knew she shouldn't worry so much about what people thought of her. It wasn't a crime to be single. It was just the more people were resigned to her singledom, it made her accept it, too. Before John, people would always ask her about her love life. At the time, the questions had annoyed her, and she had just wanted people to mind their own business. But the thing was, people expected her to meet someone. And why wouldn't they? She was a good-looking woman. Only now, she was just a lost cause. It seemed no matter how many dates that Sylvia went on she was just not clicking with anyone. Truthfully, she hadn't clicked with anyone since John.

John, the mechanic, who always smelled of grease and oil. Sylvia didn't drive. She was not interested in cars and didn't think she ever would be. John loved to talk about cars. Even when he knew it bored her to tears, he kept going on and on. He did try and refrain himself, but he just couldn't help it. When his interest had switched to motorcycles, Sylvia was happy at first. It had been good to hear him talking about something else. Until he had gone and gotten a bike and wanted her to go on spins with him. Sylvia had flat-out refused. She had no problem sitting shotgun in the car, but the bike was a death trap. She was passionate about a few things. Numbers was one of them. Hate for motorbikes was another.

She was at the Blue Velvet now. There was a small area in the front with a couple of tables and chairs placed outside. Inside was a black reception desk to her right, with a square of blue velvet stuck centre in the pane of painted wood. A tattooed woman with a bleached blonde pixie cut beamed at her. She had a menu in one hand and a pen in the other. "Are you here for the market or for food?" A smile revealed the smiley piercing above her front teeth.

"The market."

"Great stuff. It starts over there, and it continues downstairs in the basement." The woman pointed at the open doors to her right-hand side. There was a sign above the doors that said, "The Blue Ballroom."

Sylvia thanked the woman and walked in through the open doors. The stage at the back of the room was now empty. Gone were the performers, replaced with a couple of boxes that had been placed at various intervals around the stage.

There were rows and rows of stalls. Sylvia glanced at the items. There was the standard holistic stall selling crystals and incense. Sylvia walked past them. Bar a brief phase at fifteen that had terrified her very Catholic grandmother, she didn't go in for that stuff. Instead, she went straight for the clothes. There were a few items that she had spotted as soon as she entered the space. Most notable was a purple and black dress with an interesting pattern on its side.

The stallholder had long blonde hair and bore a striking resemblance to Stevie Nicks. Her accent, though, was pure Dub. All of the clothes on her stall were the kind that looked as though they were spun by edgy fairies in an enchanted woodland. The edge was what had attracted Sylvia to the black and purple dress. Although the top half of the dress was tight, the skirt part flared out and reached down to the knees. At the end of the dress was a little bit of black netting. Sylvia had a pair of high heels at home that would suit the dress perfectly.

"How much is the dress?"

"€30. Lovely, isn't it?"

Sylvia smiled. "It's gorgeous all right." A minute later she had it in her hands and was paying for it. At least she would have something nice to wear for the wedding, even if she didn't want to go to it. The Stevie Nicks-looking woman handed over a midnight blue bag and Sylvia put the dress into the bag. There were plenty of other items on the woman's stall that Sylvia wanted to buy, but she stopped herself. Years before, she had put a max of one new clothing item every time she went shopping. It had to be done after she had gone on a serious shopping haul. Jewellery and makeup didn't do anything for her, but clothes were her weakness. She should leave the market now, but there were things to buy other than clothes.

Sylvia continued browsing through the stalls before going downstairs to what was (on Friday and Saturday nights) the Blue Velvet's nightclub. It was darker here, most of its light coming from the spotlights on the ceiling with the exception of the light pouring in through the open emergency exit doors.

Despite there being a restaurant in the Blue Velvet, downstairs had several food stalls. All of them sold sweet things. Sylvia had no problem with only eating sweet things and went and bought herself a chocolate croissant. She sat on one of the benches in the centre of the room and ate it. As she ate, she perused the stalls from the bench. As well as food stalls, there were, from Sylvia's quick observation, a selection of stalls selling items that looked as though they had been chosen at random from the stallholders' houses. The only thing Sylvia liked to collect were clothes, and she had no need for anyone else's junk. No point in even searching downstairs. She'd be glad of her dress and make her way home.

She was just walking towards the stairs when a man, just above average height and with glacier blue eyes, called out to her. "Isn't it the most glorious of days that you've ever known?"

Sylvia walked over to the man. The stall was out of eyesight from the bench, and she had been far too involved with her croissant to even consider looking behind her. "It's a grand day."

"A good day for croissants?" he asked. "I saw you indulging in one from the stall across the way. You chose the right one. The other stall, the one closer to the smoking area, they're rubbish."

Sylvia saw the little stall that he was pointing at. It was just a table with a few plastic boxes with baked goods thrown inside. Something you'd glance at and forget. It was easy to forget that anything existed when standing in front of this man's stall. It was full of colour. Sylvia's eyes were dizzy with it all. She saw herbal teas, clocks, a stopwatch, a masquerade mask, and even a few potted plants.

Sylvia thought it was time to buy a new plant. It had been too long since she had treated herself to one. She had a perfect space in mind for it too: there was a table in the sitting room that was calling out for something to be added to it. She reached for the money plant.

"You know. I'm usually pretty good at reading people. I saw you coming towards me, and I thought, this is a woman who has everything in her life, but she is missing just the one thing."

"A plant," Sylvia laughed. "I'm missing a plant for my

table. Other than that, I'm flying it." Sylvia's fingertips brushed against the pot.

"This type of plant is for someone who wants to bring money into their life. And money is already something that comes easily to you. Having any more wouldn't get you any closer to what you actually want in life."

"Everyone wants more money."

"You don't."

The man was right. Money always flowed to Sylvia.

"What you need is something else. Something you've been seeking for over two years."

Sylvia's heart fluttered. "What is it that you think I'm searching for?"

"Love. Only thing missing from your life is love. The romantic type anyways."

Sylvia smiled. "Is that so?" There was a frame in the middle of the table with a hand-drawn print inside it. In the centre of the print, it said *Jackser's Bazaar*. Framing the lettering was a bell, a mask, a box of tea, and a stopwatch. Sylvia saw the print. "Is that meant to be art or is that the name of your stall?"

"Name of my stall and the name of my shop when I'm set up in a permanent fixture." He stuck out his hand.

"My name is Jackser. Welcome to my bazaar."

Sylvia shook the hand. It was cold despite how hot it was in the basement. Jackser must've been feeling the heat too if the sleeves on his rolled-up purple shirt were anything to go by. As Sylvia shook his hand, she noted an old tattoo on his left arm that looked something like a court jester. "Nice tattoo."

"Ancient old like myself. Have you had a good look around Dublin's Darling Market?"

"I have. Some lovely bits here. Even bought myself a dress for a wedding I'm going to next week."

"A wedding." Jackser's eyes widened. "How brilliant." He opened a heart-shaped purple box, revealing a selection of wedding and engagement rings. "I had someone in here only earlier today buying an engagement ring. Said he was going to bring her down to the Ha'penny Bridge tonight and propose. Very romantic, I thought."

Sylvia could see the image clearly. Her standing on the bridge with a tall, slim man on one knee before her. He was wearing a grey suit, not for the occasion, oh no, her soon-to-be fiancé would always wear suits—even on the weekends. John hated suits. No matter how fancy an event they went to, he had adamantly refused to wear one. "That's it."

"What's it?"

Sylvia grinned. All she had to do was buy an engagement ring. If she wore it to the wedding, then she could pretend that she had met someone. He wasn't at the wedding because he had been called away to an emergency somewhere…anywhere else. It was simple really. She wasn't a social media user. There would be no digital trail for people to seek out. All she would need is a picture of her and one of her male friends to show at the wedding—that was on the assumption that anyone would ask. Oh, but they would. Out of sheer curiosity, they would. It was such a simple plan. It would shut them all up. Not only was single Sylvia seeing someone, but she was engaged. The next time an event came up (maybe a year or two, plenty of time), she would have an actual partner to show off. "How much are the engagement rings?"

Jackser's head tilted to the side. "Cheapest one I have is a hundred euros." He pointed to a thin silver band with a small grey stone in the middle that, to Silvia, looked like a pebble.

"And how much is that one?" Sylvia pointed to a silver ring with a bright stone in its centre.

"€300. And it's a bargain at that. That's a real diamond. Nowhere else in the country will you see a diamond ring for this price."

Sylvia laughed. "I wouldn't know a diamond from my elbow, so you could be telling me anything, and I wouldn't have a clue. And you know that as well as I do."

"I'm no liar. But these rings aren't the right match for you. They will only repel love. If a potential suitor, at least any decent one, sees a woman with an engagement ring on then he will run to the hills, as the fella says. What you need is a ring that will bring love towards you. And for this, I have the perfect ring." Jackser reached underneath the table, where there was a stack of wooden boxes. He opened the box in the middle and took out a small pink box. "Colour of love."

"Isn't red the colour of love?" Sylvia asked.

"Red's for passion. Anger even. Pink is softer. Pink is love. And in the pink box…" Jackser opened the box revealing a gold ring with a pink stone.

Sylvia, despite her love of clothes, had never been bowled over by jewellery, but this ring was a stunner.

One that she wanted to possess. "Would I sound like Gollum if I said it's precious?"

"Not with your lovely voice. But I will warn you now that it won't make you invisible. It will make you incredibly visible. Wearing this ring will get you the love of your life."

"How would wearing a ring get you the love of your life?" Jackser still had the box open. Sylvia remembered from her teenage witchy faze that all crystals had different purposes. And rose quartz was used for love. "It's the rose quartz, isn't it? I suppose wearing it will make you think that love is on the way, so your whole vibe just changes and you're instantly more attractive."

"You know your crystals," Jackser said, impressed. He tilted his head as he thought. "I suppose the rose quartz would have something to do with it, but the other ways that this ring works..." Jackser shrugged. "Your guess is as good as mine. I'm just the middleman between seller and buyer. Many of my goods have unusual qualities. I know how to work them. I know what they do, but I don't know *how* they do what they do."

Sylvia's head was beginning to hurt. Just a little. Enough to know she really needed some fresh air and something to drink. It had been too long since she last drank anything. Her body craved something cold and sweet. But what her heart craved was the ring. Jackser handed it over to her, and Sylvia immediately slipped it on her ring finger. She felt giddy and dizzy at the feel of it.

"Anyone looking for their perfect partner just has to wear this ring and *poof*, their partner will appear."

"Where is he then?" She looked around the room. Of the few men that were currently browsing around the stall, none of them were what Sylvia deemed perfect. And the only one who was wearing a suit was Jackser himself, and he was too short and stocky to match her ideal.

"You have to write down what you want. Write down exactly what he looks like, what he wears, and what his interests are, and then, as if you've written down ingredients for your own man-shaped cake, the ring will deliver him to you."

"You sound like Jane," Sylvia said, still staring at the ring. "Except she'd call it the universe delivering the goods."

"In this case, it's a little different. You will get word-for-word what you've written. And if you don't like what you've received, then you just destroy the paper you've written the ingredients down on, and your cake will disappear. And you can start all over again."

Sylvia smiled. "And how much for this ring?"

"For you, my dear lady, €20. Not half a bad price, is it?"

"Not bad at all." Sylvia pulled a twenty from her purse and handed it over to Jackser's waiting palm. He gave her the ring's pink box. She kept the ring on her finger. Might as well leave it on and get used to the feel of it.

"Have a lovely time at your wedding, Sylvia. Just remember to wear the ring when you're writing your list. And if for whatever reason you do want to get rid of your new love, then just burn the list."

"Okay," Sylvia laughed.

Only when she was walking along the canal with an iced tea in her hand did she realise that Jackser had called her by name. And she couldn't remember telling him her name. Couldn't remember at all. Her grandfather, the man who had taught her to ride a bike and to play the tin whistle, had suffered from Alzheimer's disease. She only hoped this wasn't a sign of her going the same way. Sylvia held the cold drink against her forehead. She was being silly. She must've just told him after he introduced himself. She must've just forgotten.

When Sylvia arrived home, she hung up her new dress and left it hanging on the outside of the wardrobe. Later tonight, after she had showered, she would try it on, but she knew by looking at it that it would fit her wonderfully.

The ring was still on Sylvia's wedding finger. She wondered who else had owned it. Because it was definitely not a new ring. There were a few scratches on it already. All the more likely for her story.

She had been engaged since Christmas. It was a fast engagement after meeting at the end of August. Sylvia didn't need to think what his name was: that was easy. His name was Liam. It was a good name. A name that went well with Sylvia. Sylvia and Liam. At the wedding, she would tell them how she was beginning to give up hope when she had met Liam. He was everything that she wanted.

Sylvia went into the kitchen and took out a notepad and pen from the drawer in the television unit and brought them over to the breakfast bar. It was time, after all of

Jane's insistence, that she wrote her list.

"And what are you looking for?" She wrote his physical traits: tall, slim, dark hair, and dark eyes—that was her type. She had taken a chance with the short, blonde-haired and blue-eyed John. Then she wrote everything else she wanted in him. And after much deliberation, the list looked like this:

- He brings me croissants and iced coffee at the weekend.
- He wakes up and goes to bed at the same time as me.
- He drinks wine (red or white but never beer).
- He doesn't like sports.
- He likes all my favourite bands and reads all my favourite books.
- He wears suits all the time.
- He is neat.
- He doesn't argue and lets me make all the decisions.
- He is very sociable and wants to be out at events the whole time.
- He doesn't play video games.

- He only watches documentaries on television.

- He makes me forget about my last relationship.

Sylvia smiled. Her Liam was the opposite of John. *My Liam*. He was already feeling like her Liam. This man she didn't know. Who mightn't even exist. But the list was done.

Sylvia took out a pink-tinted glass from the cupboard and poured herself water from the tap. She sipped the water as she read through the list. If she could meet this man, then life would be perfect. Jackser had been right when he said that there was only one thing missing from Sylvia's life. And that was love—at least the romantic kind. Platonic love surrounded her in abundance. Sylvia brought the list into her bedroom and propped it in between two books: *The Magnetic Power of Not Caring* and the *Love of the Moon*. Both of them were a little hippy-dippy and both of them had been gifts from one of Sylvia's hippy friends. The books weren't bad, both of them self-help—her friends knew that she didn't read fiction. Although, really, Sylvia thought there were always elements of fiction in all the books that she read.

Especially in the new age beliefs, when everyone was just taking control of their own story.

With the list safely tucked away, Sylvia admired the dress as she ran her hand along the fabric. Her gold earrings would go wonderfully with it. Sylvia kept her barely-used jewellery in the bottom of her chest of drawers. She squatted down and opened it. There were several boxes of jewellery inside. Sylvia was reaching for the one at the back when her finger sliced against the envelope that had been there for two years. Sylvia pulled her hand out. A tear-shaped drop of blood slid down her finger.

She stood up just as there was a knock at the front door. She went into the bathroom and wrapped her finger in tissue paper. A knock again. She frowned. The only person who would ever arrive unannounced was Jane. And Sylvia knew Jane's knock. This morning it might have been "Here Comes the Bride" but usually it was some form of metal tune that Jane attempted to sound with her knuckles. The blood had already dotted through the tissue. Sylvia wrapped it one more time and then went to open the door.

The man standing outside had his fist in the air, as if

ready to knock again. He was tall, with dark brown eyes and dark hair. He smiled, revealing just a touch of dimples on each cheek. "Sylvia," he said. He held a bagged croissant in one hand and an iced coffee in the other. "Sorry I kept knocking. I was just so excited to see you." He stepped right into the hallway and wrapped his arms around Sylvia. She froze. She could feel the throbbing in her finger and smell the man's aftershave and the detergent that had been used to clean his blue suit. He handed her the coffee and croissant. "I know it's not breakfast time, but I just couldn't resist bringing them to you now."

Sylvia took the bag and the iced coffee. Her finger felt instantly better against the cold container.

"Did you hurt yourself?" he asked. He led her into the kitchen and looked around the little space. "Where do you keep the first aid box again? Of course. You moved it last week, didn't you?" He didn't wait for a reply before leaving the kitchen and going into the bathroom. His shoes, leather and shiny, made *click-clack* sounds on the wooden floor.

Sylvia had moved the first aid box. It used to be kept on the upper shelf in her wardrobe before she made space for it in the bathroom.

The man came into the room, holding the box in his hand. He set it down on the breakfast table and ordered Sylvia to take a seat. Sylvia did. Then she bolted back to her feet.

"Are you okay?" the man asked. He had a cleansing wipe in one hand and a plaster in the other.

"Who are you?" Sylvia asked.

"Who am I?" the man asked. He didn't just have dark hair; he had dark curls. He had the hint of a Greek God about him, but his accent was most definitely Irish. "Sure, I'm Liam." He held out his hands in disbelief. "Liam of the Ring."

"Liam." Sylvia stared him down from the top of his curly hair to the bottom of his shiny black shoes.

There were carving knives in the top drawer underneath the counter and one heavy statue of a Goddess (Aphrodite, bought by one of the hippy friends), and they were the lone weapons in the room. Other than that, Sylvia was on her own with a strange man that she had just let in her house. Yet she didn't feel scared. It was as though she had known this man for months.

"You can't be Liam."

"I am. You know that though, Sylvia." He held her injured finger and cleaned the wound with an antiseptic wipe, and covered it in plaster. "I think you'll be okay."

"Liam?" Sylvia whispered.

Liam smiled, setting his dimples alight. He put the empty wrappers into the bin and put the first aid kit back into the bathroom. "I'm getting a bit hungry now. Would you believe I haven't eaten anything since…well…" Liam's eyes looked up as he thought. "I don't think that I've ever eaten anything. Have I? One minute there was this rose-coloured darkness and the next, I was standing outside our door."

"Our door? This is my door. My apartment."

"Our apartment." Liam's hand dived into his pocket, and it returned with a key attached to a plastic keyring with a picture of a cat inside. It was the same keyring that Sylvia had, only her one was pink with a black cat, and his was blue with a black cat.

"How did you get that?"

"You bought it for me. Remember? When I moved in, you gave it to me?"

Sylvia did remember. Liam's lease on his flat had expired, and rather than find somewhere else to live, they had decided it would be best if he moved in.

Sylvia had cut Liam a key and attached it to the keyring and presented it to him on his first night in the apartment.

"But that didn't really happen."

"It did. Look around you; all my stuff is here."

Sylvia did. Liam, who was into modern art, had hung a print on the wall, and there were a few of his autobiographies on Sylvia's bookshelf. "How did you...how did...?"

Liam only smiled. "Remember, before I even moved in, you told me to get rid of my monster of a television? You said that there was no need for two when we already had one."

Sylvia had thought it was important to have a small television after John had insisted on having a 60-inch. Once John left, she had gotten rid of the large TV and bought the smaller one with the proceeds. "You sold your TV and with the money, we went to Galway," Sylvia said. It was there, clear in her memory.

Yet she knew it couldn't have happened. She was Sylvia, single for two years, and on intimate terms with dating sites. She was going to a wedding next weekend and using a ring to pretend she had a fiancé. The ring was on her finger. She could remember buying it from the man with the jester tattoo. But she could also remember Liam proposing to her on the Ha'penny Bridge while a tourist took pictures of them and sent her the same pictures on WhatsApp later that day. She could even remember the tourist's name: Wendy. They still texted the odd time, too.

Sylvia's phone was in her handbag. She had dumped it on her bed when she came home. She went into her bedroom. The duvet cover was different: not her usual pale yellow. Now it was white, with green elephants at the end. Sylvia's bag wasn't on the bed either. It had been placed neatly on the floor against the wall. Sylvia took the phone out. Still the same phone, but there was a crack on the screen from when she and Liam had gone out over Christmas and drank too much and Sylvia had dropped her phone on the ground. She unlocked the cracked phone and there was a picture of their engagement on the Ha'penny Bridge as her screensaver. As if that wasn't proof enough, she checked her messages and there was a whole thread from Wendy.

"Oh, shit," Sylvia said.

Liam's shoes *click-clack*ed on the floor as he entered the bedroom. "You getting hungry? I was thinking we might go out for dinner."

"Go out for dinner?" Sylvia repeated. It was Sunday night. Sundays were usually her nights to unwind and get ready for the week. It was probably the only night when she was content to just stay inside.

"Yeah, we could go over to that Italian on Thomas street? You love the pizza there." Liam smiled, and Sylvia's heart flipped. She knew the face so well now. Could remember admiring those dimples when they had first met in a lift in the St. Stephen's Green Shopping Centre. She could remember all of that, even though she knew that yesterday, he had only been a blur in her mind. A vague shape of what her ideal man would look and act like. Sylvia opened her wardrobe and saw half of it was filled with Liam's suits. Different colours and materials, but all of them beautiful.

"Unless you want to go somewhere else? I genuinely don't mind," Liam said.

"Pizza sounds wonderful."

Sylvia put on a knee length yellow dress and checked her

reflection in the mirror on the back of the wardrobe door. She smiled. The yellow dress always made her happy, even during that bad time after John left. She opened her jewellery drawer and took out the box that contained the pearl necklace. Her fingers brushed against the envelope that had injured her earlier.

Sylvia took the pearls out of the box and brought them into the living area. Liam was reading *How Far the Light Reaches*. Sylvia had only just finished it herself. In the Liamless life, she had left it on a table by the door, intending to bring it to one of her colleagues, but in this life, she could remember Liam asking if he could read it when she was done. "You enjoying the book?" Sylvia asked.

"It's good." Liam saw the pearls in her hand, stood up, and fastened them around her neck. The pearls felt silky and smooth on Sylvia's skin. "You look beautiful. I love this dress on you."

"You've seen me wearing it before?" Sylvia asked.

"Of course. You wore it when we went to the National Concert Hall. Remember?"

Sylvia remembered the two of them sitting side-by-side in the stalls. Afterwards, they had gone for cocktails and got far too drunk. At least Sylvia had. Liam could hold his drink to the point that he always looked sober. "That was a few months ago, wasn't it?"

"It sure was. Just before October." He smiled at her before bending down and kissing her. He really was tall. Probably the tallest man that Sylvia had ever kissed, never mind lived with or been engaged to. All of these memories. Pity it felt like only half of her had been there when the memories were made.

"Where did you get the engagement ring from?" Sylvia asked. She twisted the ring once around her finger. It was a good fit. She would hate for it to fall off and for Liam and these lovely memories to just disappear.

"It was in Galway, when we went on holiday with the money from the TV sale, remember? It was some vintage place that sold clothes, too. That man Jackser ran it."

"Jackser's Bazaar?" Sylvia asked.

"That's the place. He's an odd man, Jackser."

Jackser had been at Dublin's Darling Market. Sylvia remembered him there. Or maybe it was a dream. The more Sylvia thought about it, the more likely it seemed. On Sunday, she and Liam went to Phoenix Park to burn off the weekend calories. "This is going to sound mad, but when are we getting married again?"

"May the first. Remember, on Bealtaine? The festival of love?"

Sylvia laughed. "You know me; when I'm hungry, I can hardly think straight." She put on her shoes, and they left the apartment.

"How is the lovely couple this evening?" the server in the Italian asked.

"We are great." Liam said.

"Certainly are," Sylvia agreed.

Liam tightened his hold on her hand as they walked to a table by the window and sat down. They ordered white wine and margherita pizza. The wine came and they sipped it.

"How's your finger feeling now?" Liam asked.

The only part of it that hurt now was the tightness of the plaster. She wanted to go into the bathroom and rip it off. "It feels grand. Imagine only a papercut could do that?"

"Paper can be dangerous. You'd want to be careful."

The pizza came and it was delicious. It always was from there. She'd first tasted it during her Christmas work-do. That night, all she had wanted was someone to go home to. Yet that had only been the Christmas just gone, and Liam had been waiting for her at home.

"Are you alright?" Liam asked as he was splitting the last slice of pizza in two. "You look confused about something."

"We were together at Christmas, weren't we?" Sylvia asked. "We didn't break up or anything?"

"No. We were together as we are now." He put half the slice on Sylvia's plate. Drizzles of pesto dripped down its side. Sylvia scraped them off with the edge of her fork. "I came here for my work Christmas party, didn't I?"

"You did. And I met you afterwards, and we went to the Brazen Head with your work friends."

Sylvia could see that clearly. Liam had worn a wine-coloured suit with a black shirt and a white tie, and he had spent the night charming everyone there. They all loved him.

"I think I must be getting confused with the year before then," Sylvia said, even though there hadn't been a party the year before on account of COVID. It could've been pre-COVID times, though. That was probably it.

After they had eaten, Liam paid for the food and left a generous tip for the service staff. They walked hand-in-hand down Francis Street and went into the Liberty Bell. They stopped there for a few glasses of white before continuing into town. Sylvia felt like such a rebel.

They arrived home after midnight. Sylvia remembered drinking water and then slipping into bed, but that was about it. She had lost her memory somewhere on Camden Street.

***

When her alarm went off the next day, she had a sore head and dry mouth.

Liam must've felt the same way, if his red eyes and pasty skin were anything to go by. "Morning," he said as he yawned. "It was a good night last night, wasn't it?"

Sylvia agreed that it was. She slowly got out of bed, wishing that she had been asleep an hour before midnight. She went into the kitchen and poured herself a glass of water.

After a shower and drinking water, Sylvia did feel somewhat better. Liam kissed her goodbye, and she went out into the beautiful day.

Even with the hangover, Sylvia could see life was good. She was a lucky woman. She had a wonderful fiancé, a job she loved, and amazing friends. And there was the wedding at the weekend. There, she could finally show Liam off to her old school friends. They were just going to love him. Everyone loved Liam; what was not to love?

By home time, grogginess had replaced the hangover. Sylvia was mid-yawn when she went into her apartment and saw Liam. He was wearing one of his black suits.

"How was your day?" he asked as he took off his suit jacket and draped it across the armchair. Sylvia remembered dating a man once years before who used to throw his jacket onto the sofa—it used to drive her mad.

"Really great." And it was, despite the hangover , it had been a wonderful day.

"You're still up for going out tonight?" Liam asked.

"Of course."

After dinner, they changed and left for the pub. The lift was in use, so they walked down the stairs. They met Jane on the second floor. She had her earplugs in, and metal music streamed out. She removed them and said hello. She glanced at Liam but kept her eyes trained on her friend.

"It feels like yesterday, but it's been weeks, hasn't it?" Sylvia asked.

"It has." Jane shuffled on her feet and glanced at the stairs behind Sylvia. "I've been on lots of hikes recently."

"We should go with you. Liam would only love going on a hike, wouldn't you?"

"Absolutely." Liam's dimples were fully engaged now. "That would be some laugh."

"Well, I better get moving." Jane brushed past them and continued up the stairs. "Good to see you."

"We are going over to Sullivan's. Do you want to come with us? Sonny from downstairs is playing his first—"

"I'm all good. Got a few things to do tonight. I'll catch you another time." She walked away and slipped her headphones into her ear.

Sylvia watched her go before turning around to Liam, who was smiling as usual. "That's so strange. She's always mad to go to Sullivan's with me."

"Is she?" Liam asked. "She only came once with us."

Sylvia bit her thumbnail. She had already chewed off some of the fresh varnish. "It must've been before we met then."

"Must've been."

Sylvia and Liam walked across the road to Sullivan's and took a seat towards the front of the bar, where they watched Sonny sing folk songs and play his guitar. The pub was neither too big nor too small, and, barring the midst of summer, there was always a fire burning in the hearth. The fire burning that night was small. There was no real need for one, but it was nice to look at it. When Sonny took a short break, they watched the flames and made out shapes in the fire.

"I see a glass. A glass filled with gin and tonic."

"That's a hint, if ever there was one." Liam went over to the bar. There was a crowd gathered in front of it, but it shifted quickly. Sylvia watched Liam order their drinks and she admired him when he sat back down. He placed a gin and tonic on the beer mat in front of her and wine on his own mat.

"You always drink wine."

"I do. Can't stand anything else other than water." At that, he *clink*ed his glass against her own and they toasted the rest of the night.

***

Liam came into the room as Sylvia zipped her skirt. He had a towel wrapped around his middle and a toothbrush in his hand. "You're going to be late if you don't leave soon," he said.

Sylvia yawned. "I'm just so tired. These late nights are killing me. I'm going to have to go to sleep earlier."

"Really?" Liam asked. "It's never affected you like this before. I hope you're not sick."

"I always go to sleep early. You know what I'm like."

Liam shrugged. "We always go out just about every night, remember?"

Sylvia saw the blur of parties that had already been. She and Liam were social butterflies. Going everywhere they were invited. Always busy and always together. "I remember. Maybe it's old age catching up with me. I probably just need to start sleeping earlier now."

"Okay," Liam said. The dimples were back, shining full and deep. "If that's what you need."

Sylvia knew that was what she needed, yet she didn't resist the opportunity to go out that very same night when Liam suggested it. Nothing crazy, he had promised. It was just an exhibition at one of the local galleries. Sylvia was ecstatic when he told her about the event. She had planned on watching documentaries for the evening, but they seemed so dull in comparison.

"We don't have to go, of course. I just said I'd say it to you."

There was no way Sylvia was going to let the opportunity slip by. "Not a hope."

They went. Yet again, it was another great night.

The next night, Sylvia knew she had to start taking things easy. So instead of taking Liam up on his offer to go out for dinner, she asked if they could stay at home.

"Of course, we can stay at home. We can do anything you want to do."

"Great. We can watch that new series on the Amazon rainforest."

"Sounds wonderful."

"You don't mind staying in?"

"I don't mind if that's what you want."

When Sylvia sat on the couch, he joined her on the opposite side, and they watched half of the first episode before the rumbling in Sylvia's stomach was too much to ignore. "What do you want for dinner?"

"How about we order food?"

"Or just throw on some pasta?"

"That sounds even better."

And that was their evening. They ate pasta. Nothing fancy, just some fusilli, with sauce bought in Lidl, frozen vegetables, and cheese melted on the top. After watching two episodes of the documentary series, they read their books until it was time to go to bed.

Feeling well-rested, the following night Sylvia went for a few drinks in the local where they had watched Sonny do his show. There was no performer that night.

"It's not the same without Sonny here, is it? Or anyone singing, for that matter."

"It's not. You're absolutely right." He drank from his glass of white wine.

"Do you know which suit you're going to wear for the wedding?"

"Still the purple one. Remember, we talked about it?"

Sylvia's temple throbbed. She rubbed it, and the pain eased. "I think I remember." But when she searched inside her head, there was only blankness. She remembered her dress—the one that she was going to wear. She had only bought it at the place when she had gone on Sunday. The Sunday just before. "Where did I buy my purple dress?"

"Oh," Liam said, searching the empty stage before shrugging. "You came home from work last week with it. I think maybe that shop in George's Street Arcade?"

"That must've been it." She could just about see herself strolling in there and browsing through the racks of dresses. "Anyways, your suit's going to look great with my dress." She took his hands and held them in her own. "I can't wait to bring you to the wedding. Everyone's going to love you."

***

The next morning, she was fresh and ready for the day. Sylvia was going to meet Liam at Heuston after work. She would change into jeans in the bathrooms at work before leaving. She added her travel clothes and zipped the suitcase. Despite only bringing the bare essentials, she still had to hold the suitcase down to close it.

Liam had his own suitcase on the bed. His purple suit was in, neatly folded, but that was all that had been packed. He didn't have to leave the apartment as early as Sylvia did. He had all the time in the world, he assured her.

"You all good to go?" Liam came into the bedroom with his travel toiletry bag. He was all suited and booted, looking extremely dapper today in his navy suit.

"Just there now. And I'll see you at Heuston after work?"

"You will indeed." Liam walked her to the door and kissed her.

Only after the door had closed and Sylvia was on her way with her suitcase bobbing behind her did she realise that she had absolutely no idea what Liam worked at. How could she not know? They were engaged. They lived together. She must know. Maybe it was one of those things that she had forgotten. She was forgetting so many things these days.

She scratched her chin. The other man used to scratch his chin all the time. It was a trait she had stolen from him. And he had stolen her heart.

Liam waited in front of Heuston Station. He kissed Sylvia, and she wanted to rub the kiss away and immediately felt guilty. She shouldn't feel like that. This was her Liam. The man she had agreed to marry.

They went inside. It was noisy and thronged with people all wanting to leave Dublin.

"Are you hungry?" Liam asked. "I'm hungry."

"You're always hungry."

Liam laughed. "I suppose I am. Where will we eat then?"

"Where do you want to eat?" Sylvia asked.

"Wherever you want," Liam said.

Sylvia scanned the Arrivals and Departures boards. Their train was leaving in twenty minutes, but it would board in ten. Even if she wanted to dine-in, they were too pushed for time to do so. "We'll just get a sandwich. We can go out to eat when we get to Tramore."

"Okay," Liam said. He was smiling. "Sounds good to me."

Sylvia curled her lip. The one before, the one she couldn't remember, used to fight her on just about everything, but they always reached a decision in the end. She inwardly scolded herself. She shouldn't be comparing Liam to someone.

They bought a takeaway sandwich each and hot drinks from Bewley's and then waited for the train. There was already a large queue of people ahead of them. Some wore suits, and some were country shoppers for the day, going on a daytrip to Dublin.

The boarding of the train began, and people shuffled

forwards. Liam beamed down at her. "This is going to be great," he said.

Sylvia wasn't sure if he meant the train or the wedding, or just getting away for the weekend. "It sure is," she said.

They arrived on their carriage, took their assigned seating, and ate their sandwiches. Sylvia hadn't noticed it before, but Liam ate like a mouse, taking little nibbles and looking around guiltily as if at any moment he would be caught and the food would be taken away.

"It's a great sandwich," Liam said. "Probably the best one that I've ever had."

"It was grand," Sylvia said. She took out her book and began reading.

"Great idea," Liam said. He took out his own book from his satchel. Neither of them put down their books until they reached Waterford.

When they arrived, they got into one of the available taxis waiting outside the front. Sylvia sat in the passenger seat, and Liam sat in the back, looking far too large for the space. The ginger taxi man had the bushiest moustache that Sylvia had ever seen. He only asked the obligatory questions and stayed quiet for the rest of the ride.

Liam was gazing at everything as the taxi drifted into Tramore. His smile was ever-present.

Sylvia looked to her left and saw the sea at the end of the road. It was just a calm-looking blue line, but up close, it could be roaring.

The taxi dropped them off in front of a large white hotel with a selection of flags on the poles outside. Sylvia and Liam went to the reception and checked in. The hotel had three floors of upstairs accommodation. Their room was situated on the top floor. They took the lift and went to their bedroom. Like the exterior, it was painted white. The bed linen on the king-sized bed was white, too. The pillows strewn on top were the same blue as the sea that could be seen directly outside the balcony door. Sylvia set down her little suitcase and opened the doors. Sea air filled her lungs. There were two plastic seats and a plastic table on the balcony. Away in the distance, the sun was beginning to set, but there was still another half an hour of light left in the sky.

"Would you like to get some fresh air?" Sylvia asked. "Maybe get a walk in before the sun goes down for the night?"

"What would you like to do?" Liam asked.

"Go for a walk," Sylvia said. "Maybe get some dinner then before coming back."

Liam smiled. "If that's what you want, then that sounds wonderful to me."

"Is that what you want?" Sylvia asked. "You don't just want to stay here and maybe get some room service?"

"I want whatever you want to do," Liam said.

Sylvia frowned. Her chest tightened. She got up from her seat. "Well, let's go then," she said. "Let's just bloody go."

"Are you alright, Sylvia?" Liam asked.

"Fine," Sylvia said.

They left the hotel and walked along the mostly deserted beach. There were only a few lone dog walkers out there, and a handful of people were swimming in the sea. Sylvia's grandparents used to bring her to the beach when she was a child.

Her mother never did. Mostly Sylvia and her mother stayed at home. Usually, Sylvia was somewhere watching television or keeping quiet in her room. Her bedroom was the only place in the house guaranteed to be clean. Sometimes the rest of the house was decent, but other times it was covered with beer cans, glass bottles and butts. It just depended on how her mother was feeling.

On the day that she left, the house had been spotless. It was the cleanest that Sylvia had ever seen it. She thought her mother must have been in an excellent mood if the house was that clean, and that they would get to order the chipper for dinner and even get a Vienetta for afterwards. Her heart had still been singing when she opened the envelope, and it sliced the edge of her finger, and blood dripped onto the paper.

"Do you like the sea?" Liam asked.

"Yes," Sylvia said. Its temperament used to remind her of her mother: sometimes calm and sometimes volatile. But at least the sea was always there. It might run away from you, but it would always come back. "Do you?" Sylvia asked.

"Of course I do," Liam said.

Sylvia nodded. Of course, he did. Why wouldn't he? If she liked it, then he did, too.

***

Sylvia woke to her alarm. She had put it on the other side of the room the previous evening, so neither she nor Liam would oversleep. They had gone to a Chinese restaurant in the end. A suggestion that Liam had readily agreed to. Sylvia was beginning to think that if she asked Liam if he wanted earthworms, he would eat the worms.

"Good morning," Liam said.

"Morning." Sylvia went to the balcony doors. The sun was bright and brilliant. Lisa and Fred would have a beautiful day. Sylvia didn't know Fred well; she'd only met him a handful of times. The last was in September at their mutual friend's baby's christening.

"Liam, why is it again that you weren't with me in September for the christening?" When she tried to think, her mind gifted her a blank.

Liam came over to the door and placed his palm on the glass. "Oh, I was scheduled for a business trip at work. I tried to get out of it, but there was no way around it, remember?"

Sylvia nodded. She checked the time on her watch. It was already ten. She yawned, even though she had had plenty of sleep.

Liam's suit was the same shade of purple as Sylvia's dress. Everyone told Sylvia how well the two of them looked together. Liam, for his part, was charming and lovely with Sylvia's friends. By the end of the evening, she had a multitude of people telling her how much they loved her new beau. Lisa was among them.

"It would be even better if the two of ye left Dublin and came home to live." Lisa's hair, which had been immaculate at the ceremony, was now loose with flyaway strands sticking out this way and that, and her bright wedding dress had drops of red wine on its front.

"Or you and Fred come and live in Dublin," Sylvia said. "Much more to do in Dublin."

Lisa laughed. "There's some chance of that alright. Really though I miss seeing you. You know the last time I saw you was with John." Lisa cleared her throat. "Oh no, it was the christening. I completely forgot about it. I was a bit pissed, though, to be fair." Her eyes sought the bar at the back of the room. There was a crowd of people gathered around it. "I'd murder a vodka and coke; would you like something?"

Sylvia was drinking the wine that had been served with dinner. She held up the half-full glass. "I've still got this."

Lisa placed a hand on the top of Sylvia's arm. "I'll talk to you later."

Sylvia drank from her wine and watched Lisa walk

over to the bar with the bouquet hanging limply at her side. Immediately, the bride was swarmed by people.

Gradually each person disappeared until all Sylvia could see was a man slightly shorter than average. He had blonde hair and blue eyes that shone from either happiness or the beer that was in his hands. He was laughing at something, someone, a ghost maybe because Sylvia couldn't see anyone standing with him.

"John," Sylvia said. She took two steps towards the man before he disappeared. Liam came behind Sylvia and hugged her. It was too tight. She struggled for breath.

"Are you okay, Sylvia?" he asked. "Are you okay?"

Sylvia pushed his hands away and ran outside. The sky was drunk with stars. Pink clouds stroked the line above the sea. Sylvia took a deep breath. Her lungs burned. She walked around the little garden in front of the hotel and willed herself to calm down. "John," she whispered. He had been with her here two years ago at a wedding. They had been together for years and she had forgotten his name.

"There you are," Liam said. He had loosened the top of his shirt. "Are you alright?"

"Grand," she said. "I just needed air, that's all. It was

getting a bit hot inside. I'll go back now and get a drink."

She walked into the ballroom. Liam followed and attempted to lead her onto the dance floor. She shook him off and refused all invitations to dance with him for the rest of the evening.

**

Sunlight streamed in through the window. It burned Sylvia's eyes. She opened them and turned around to see Liam.

"Good morning, sunshine," he said.

There was a throbbing pain between Sylvia's eyes. It felt as though there was something behind the skin kicking, attempting to break free. She closed her eyes, but it did little to alleviate the pain.

"Do you've a hangover?" Liam asked.

"What gave it away?" Sylvia always kept Panadol in the front compartment of her suitcase for emergencies. She popped two from the foil and swallowed them with a glass of water.

On the train, Sylvia nibbled a flapjack that she had picked up at the shop in the train station.

"How are you feeling now?" Liam asked.

"I'm fine," Sylvia said. She closed her eyes and dropped her head against the seat. At the Kilkenny station, two people got onto the train. They, too, had left Dublin for the weekend. Unlike Sylvia or Liam, they had thick Dublin accents. Their weekend had been pretty standard from what Sylvia could hear. The conversation bored her terribly until she found out that the man's name was Jack. Sylvia peeped through the gap in the chairs. She saw a woman and a man, both in their sixties, with reddish cheeks. The woman had narrow green eyes while the man's were obscenely blue and bulging.

Liam was reading a book. One that Sylvia had finished on Friday evening. "You're awake," he said. "Did you have a nice sleep?" He set the book down on the table.

"I bought my dress in Dublin's Darling Market," she said. "I did; I know I did. And the man was called Jackser. He sold me this ring." She held up her hand. The engagement ring was heavy on her finger.

"I bought you that ring from a man called Jackser," Liam said.

"You bought it?" Sylvia asked. "You sure that you bought it?"

"Of course, I did," Liam said. "Remember the trip to

Galway? Remember me proposing to you on the Ha'penny Bridge? Remember?"

Sylvia's heart raced. She placed her hand over it. "I went to Dublin's Darling Market on Sunday last week, I did. And I bought the dress—the purple dress—from Jackser, and he was wearing a purple suit."

Liam took Sylvia's trembling hand in his own. "You always get like this the next day after you've drank too much. You always do. Remember?"

Sylvia bit her cheek and tasted iron inside her mouth. She took a drink of water. It was true that her hangovers could be cruel. She took after her mother in that regard. A good drinking bout could leave her exhausted.

Liam squeezed her hand, causing the bones inside to make crunching sounds. "Don't stress yourself out so much. You're only upsetting yourself. You bought the dress in Galway. I bought your engagement ring from Jackser in his bazaar. We didn't go to Dublin's Darling Market. I know you wanted to go. We agreed to go the next time, remember?"

"Okay," Sylvia said.

Liam held the apartment door open for Sylvia. She

thanked him and rolled her suitcase into the bedroom, and left it on the floor.

Liam eyed her discarded suitcase. "Aren't you going to unpack?" he asked.

"Sure, we're only back," Sylvia said. "There's plenty of time."

"Whatever you like," Liam said.

Sylvia went into the kitchen and walked around the apartment. She remembered cooking breakfast last Sunday. Remembered sitting at the breakfast bar on her own when there was a knock at the door. Sylvia placed her palm on the counter. There had been a leaflet there. A leaflet for Dublin's Darling Market.

"What would you like for dinner?" Liam called from the bedroom.

"Whatever you want," Sylvia said.

She could hear Jane's footsteps upstairs. Sylvia left the apartment and knocked on Jane's door.

Somewhere downstairs, she could hear Liam calling out, "Sylvia? Sylvia?"

"Sylvia?" Jane echoed. "Are you okay?"

Sylvia went into Jane's apartment and closed the door behind her. Sylvia held her finger against her lips. "I don't want him to know I'm here."

"Is everything alright?" Jane asked, keeping her voice low. "Did he hurt you?"

"No," Sylvia said. "Nothing like that. I just need a minute to clear my head."

Jane led Sylvia into the kitchen. Jane's dinner of noodles and veg sizzled on the frying pan. "Are you hungry?" Jane asked.

"I'm okay, Sylvia said. Jane had a small kitchen table and chairs; Sylvia sat down and rubbed her hand against her head. On top of the table was the leaflet for Dublin's Darling Market. It was the same leaflet that Sylvia remembered sitting on top of her countertop.

"Did you have this in my flat?" Sylvia asked.

"The what?" Jane asked.

Sylvia picked up the leaflet. "This," she said.

"No," Jane said. "You must've got one through the post, perhaps?"

"I remember you coming into my place last Sunday with this in your hand. You left it on the counter."

Jane shook her head.

Sylvia closed her eyes. "Maybe I'm going mad then. It would have to be that, wouldn't it?"

"Maybe you were dreaming?"

"You don't come to my place anymore, do you? You used to before Liam moved in. You used to come for cups of tea the whole time. I know you're busy with Leonie but it would be nice to see more of you. I miss us hanging out."

"I…you're welcome here anytime you like; you know that. I've said it to you loads of times."

Sylvia couldn't remember that at all. "You don't like Liam, is that it?"

Jane nodded. "I'm sorry, Sylvia. I really don't. I can't even stand being in the same room as him." Jane scratched her teeth against her bottom lip. "What's the deal with the suits? He wears them the whole time, but I've never seen him go to work. Unless, is he working from home? Every time I ask him, he changes the subject."

"I don't know what he does."

"How can you seriously marry a man and you've no idea what he does for a living? Oh God, you don't think he works for some secret government agency or something. Are there jobs even like that in Ireland? Sure, there'd have to be. Wouldn't there?"

Sylvia ran her hand against the leaflet. She had gone. She had been looking for a dress for the wedding. She had been in a strange humour because she knew she would be going alone and…Sylvia stood up. "I went to that market; I did go to the market."

"I'm sorry," Jane said. "Did I go too far?"

"No." Sylvia remembered it all now. Remembered buying the ring from Jackser and remembered him telling her to make a list while wearing the ring. And there had been something else. A way to get rid of the love interest. All Sylvia had to do was burn the page.

"Are you okay, Sylvia?" Jane asked. There was a deep frown line on her forehead.

Sylvia nodded. "When I see you again, things will be different." She hugged Jane and left the apartment before Jane could say anything. How deranged she must have looked. Maybe she was. Maybe she had lost the plot and was simply imagining everything. How likely was it that a ring could summon up a man from the page? Yet that was what happened. Sylvia was sure of it. She hadn't brought the apartment key with her when she had left, so she knocked on the door. Liam opened it a moment later.

"Sylvia," he said. "I was so worried. Are you okay?

Where did you go?" He attempted to hug her, but Sylvia dived out of the way. She went into the kitchen. Liam had left a book face down on the breakfast bar.

"What's wrong?" Liam asked. He gripped her shoulders. "Sylvia, what's wrong?"

Sylvia pushed the hands away. "I know what you are," she said. "I remember everything now."

"I'm me. I'm Liam."

"Liam of the Ring," she said, holding up the finger with the ring on it. "You'd think I'd forget."

"Oh, Sylvia," Liam said. "It has to be a hangover. There's no other reason why you'd be acting like this."

"I bought the ring from Jackser. He told me I had to make a list of all the qualities I wanted in a partner. He said if I did so while wearing the ring, then that person would come into my life. And you appeared then. You came to the door with the iced coffee and the croissants."

"I bring you iced coffee and croissants at the weekend," Liam nodded. "It's kind of my thing to do."

"Because I wrote it like that. I wrote it on the list." She spotted the book that Liam had been reading. "The books," she exclaimed. That had been it. That had been where she had left it: propped between two books on the bookshelf in her room. She went into her bedroom and pulled out the *Magnetic Power of Not Caring* and *The Power of the Moon*, but there was no slip of paper. "It was here," she said. "I know that I left it here."

Liam was staring at her with his eyebrow raised. "Where is it then?" he asked. "Where is the paper?" He took off his suit jacket and unbuttoned the top two buttons on his shirt. "Would you like a glass of water? Flush out all of the toxins in your body, and I bet you'll feel so much better. You often get like this after drinking, remember? Just like your mother."

"I'm nothing like my mother!" Sylvia opened the books and fruitlessly searched through the pages.

Liam watched her.

"Where did you put it?" Sylvia asked. Her voice was calm, but her hands were shaking.

"There's no list, Sylvia."

"You hid it." Sylvia's eyes were red. Tears ran down her face.

Liam shook his head. "You're having an episode. You're having one of your episodes. You have them sometimes, remember?"

"No, I don't," Sylvia shouted. She pulled heaps of

books from the shelf and combed through them. Nothing. Sylvia searched the room, looking in and under every and anything.

"It's not here, Sylvia. You know it's not. And you know why? Because it doesn't even exist. This happened before with you, remember?"

Sylvia brushed past him and went into the kitchen. She examined the small collection of books in there, but again, her search yielded nothing. Liam watched with a little smile on his face.

His smirk was suffocating. She needed air. Her apartment keys were in a glass bowl on the counter; she grabbed them and ran out of the door and down the stairs. Each step away from Liam let the tightness in her chest ease. Liam of the fucking ring.

Sylvia opened the front door and walked out into the evening. Away from Liam, she could catch her breath. She took the ring off her finger and put it in her pocket. It was madness to wear it. Maybe now everything would return to normal, but Sylvia knew that wasn't true. Jackser had told her she would need to burn the list to rid herself of her creation. Without the list, how could she get rid of him? If she destroyed the ring, perhaps? There was an ironmonger across the road. Sylvia could ask them to melt it and see if that did anything.

Sylvia was just going to cross the road when the motorbike whizzed past. She stopped at the edge of the footpath. John's motorbike looked just like it. She did try and make him get rid of it. There had been a fight. Just a small one.

The final fight had been a big one. It started not over the motorbike but the television. That stupid, oversized television. Sylvia had wanted him to downsize it. To buy one that didn't look humongous in their little living space.

Sylvia had left the apartment with her face boiling. When she had returned, an envelope waited for her on the bed. She sat and held it in her hands, staring at the paper, wondering what it would say. John had known her mother had left but he didn't know about the envelope on the mantelpiece. Her phone was beside her on the bed. When it rang, Sylvia picked it up. Not checking the name, only hoping it would say John, she put the phone to her ear. There came the news. A motorbike accident. The end of a young life. The envelope had sat on the bedside table for months afterwards before it was buried in the drawer.

Sylvia turned on her heel. Back up to the apartment.

Liam needed the list to live. There was only one place that he'd think she wouldn't search.

She marched up the stairs and opened her apartment door. Liam was there. Smiling at her. "Sylvia, I missed you."

Sylvia went into the bedroom she had shared with John, the room he spent his final night on earth, and she locked the door.

Liam rattled the handle. "Sylvia," he said. "Why are you locking the door?"

Sylvia sank to her knees and opened the bottom drawer. The letter was there. No longer pristine but stained with tears and the blood that she had shed on it a week ago.

The doorknob went from side to side.

Sylvia sat on her bed—back to the place where she had found the envelope two years before. Her hands shook as she opened it. Inside were two pieces of paper: her list and the other, John's letter. Sylvia had no idea how Liam put the list in there. It didn't matter. She ripped up her list, and Liam's prattling outside the door ceased.

Somewhere outside, an emergency siren sang.

Sylvia read through John's letter. The first and last one

he had ever written to her. This was what it said:

Dear Sylvia,

Let's get a smaller TV. It does look too big. I'm going for a spin to Wicklow. See you tonight. I love you.

John

That was it. Nothing scary. Not a breakup, as she had feared for the last two years. He had loved her, and he had been planning on coming home. Why he had felt the need to write that down and not just send a text message was a mystery. Or why not just leave a note? Why go the whole hog and use an envelope, too? Sylvia didn't know. She would never know.

A knock on the front door. Sylvia wasn't going to answer it until she heard the tune of "For Whom the Bell Tolls." She unlocked her bedroom door.

No sign of Liam. He was gone.

Another knock on the front door. Sylvia opened it. Jane stood outside. Her face was red from running. There was a sweatband around her forehead. She barged straight through, went into the kitchen, and poured herself a glass of water. "Sorry," she said through a mouthful of water. "I was gasping. So how was the wedding?"

"The wedding?" Sylvia said.

"Yeah, the wedding. You know the one you just came back from?"

New memories were in Sylvia's head now. Faint. More like a dream. She had drunk wine and danced and had a wonderful time. All by herself. "Great," she said. "It was great."

"Did you tell people you were engaged?" Jane asked.

"I told you about that plan, did I?"

"You did indeed," Jane said.

A whoosh of the previous week's memories came back. The week that Sylvia had not had. A week without Liam, when the ring was just a ring. Sylvia met Jane's eyes. "I have to tell you something. Something I've been hiding. John, my ex, he…I didn't want to talk about it before. I just called him my ex but he's dead. We didn't break up. He died."

"I know," Jane said. "One of the other neighbours told me. I figured you just didn't want to talk about it."

"I thought he had broken up with me." Sylvia told her about the envelope. And the first envelope that her mother had left all those years before. "I thought he was leaving just like her. I thought it was a goodbye. But it wasn't."

After Jane went home, Sylvia put on her shoes and walked down to the Liffey. It wasn't far. The canal was nearer, but the Liffey was stronger. It, she knew, would love the ring. The last of the sunlight disappeared from the day; now only the night glimmered on the river's surface. She leaned over the side and threw the ring into it.

PADDY'S DAY

The mannequins in the charity shop window were dressed for the occasion. One wore a dress, and the other wore a blazer with corduroy trousers. All of the clothes were various shades of green, and both mannequins had on Paddy caps. On the windows were shamrock stickers and little pots of gold.

Maria, who volunteered in the shop with Paddy, had done the window display. She'd said the shamrocks would bring them all a bit of luck.

The first thing Paddy saw after Jim had decked him were the shamrocks. He didn't feel lucky then. Not in the least. Later on, when the shock had worn off, Paddy counted that it was luck that the off-duty Garda called into the shop just as Jim was getting his knuckles bloody.

If that hadn't happened, then Paddy would've received more than a black eye.

Angela, a regular who came in every Wednesday and Friday, plopped her items on the counter. She was all smiles before she saw Paddy's bruise. "Jesus Christ, Paddy, what's after happening to your face?" Her hair was pixie short and peroxide blonde. The bones on her body looked sharp and cutting.

"My face has always been like this, but the black eye is a new look that I've been trying out. I think it adds something to my face, wouldn't you say?" Paddy grinned. No point in telling her that his girlfriend's ex had done the damage. Although by now, half the town already knew. The joys of having one of the town's gossips perusing through the racks when Jim stormed in through the door.

Angela shook her head. "Have you had it looked at?"

"No need. It's already nothing compared to how it looked yesterday." Paddy wasn't sure how true that was but optimism was always the way forward.

"Do you mind me asking what happened? It wasn't a robbery, was it?" Angela moved closer to him, her eyes hungry.

"A disgruntled customer. Wasn't impressed when I wouldn't give him a discount. It's the dangers of volunteering in a charity shop. What can I say?"

"Did they catch him?" Angela glanced at the security camera above the till. There was another one at the far end of the shop that surveyed the rest of the small space.

"Will I tell you a secret?" Paddy leaned towards Angela. "Those cameras haven't been working since October. The manager keeps promising to do something about them, but she never does. But enough about me and my mug. What are you doing on this lovely St. Patrick's Day? Are you going to see the parade?"

"I'm not," Angela said. "I've bought a few bits for the garden. I'll get a bit of work done on it." Angela rubbed her chin. "Your eye really looks awful."

"Ah it'll be grand," Paddy said. "Don't you be worrying about me."

Paddy sorted through Angela's finds. There were two Aran jumpers, a Pilates DVD, and a book on gardening. He entered the items into the till and told her the price.

"You've gave me a discount again. You're as good to be doing it."

"Sure you're my favourite customer. And you're

always in buying your bits."

"Are you in here for the day?"

"Always am. Black eye or not."

"I thought maybe on account of it being St. Patrick's Day, then ye might close early."

Paddy put Angela's purchases into a paper bag and placed the bag to the side. "Not at all. Full day as always. Got to keep the money rolling in for the animals."

Angela smiled. "Well, I hope you've a good day, and that eye clears up soon enough."

"You and me both." Paddy winked at Angela with his good eye. "I don't think the thug look is doing me any favours. And I'm meeting the girlfriend's parents later."

"You are?"

"First time meeting them and look at the cut of me."

Angela's phone rang inside her handbag. She glanced at the bag and rolled her eyes. "Probably work seeing if I can come in. I'll see you next week."

Paddy waved goodbye. He winced when Angela let the door fall behind her and the glass rattled in the pane.

"Who's banging the door?" Maria came out of the stockroom at the back of the shop. She had several jumpers on hangers. "One of these days that glass is going to shatter, and then we'll have a lawsuit on our hands. As well as a black eye." Maria frowned when she looked at Paddy. "Any news from the guards on that Jim fella?"

"None," Paddy said. "He'll get another restraining order and that'll be that."

The door opened. Laura, a blonde in her late twenties, walked into the shop. She wore a green wool coat that reached to her knees. "It looks even worse," she said. She went over to Paddy and held his face in her hands before kissing him.

"It's grand," Paddy said. "By tomorrow you won't even be able to see it." Paddy went out from behind the counter. "I'll take my hour now, Maria. If you get any bother, give us a buzz and I'll come back."

"Go on," Maria said, waving him away.

"Just ring if you need anything." Paddy held the door open for Laura and let it close gently behind him. Outside, they could hear the faint sound of a brass band playing. As they walked away from the side street where the charity shop was located and turned onto Main Street, the sound grew louder. At the top of Main Street, the band played on a stage that was set up just for the day's activities. A group of people gathered around the band. Further up the road, people in costumes gave out sweets to children and money-off vouchers for various shops around the town to the adults.

Paddy and Laura continued walking until they came to a large building that used to be a carpet store before closing down. It was now used as a space for Sunday markets and craft fairs. Paddy himself wasn't a fan of perusing through the stalls, unlike Laura, who never left without picking up one or two things.

"It's a way of supporting local businesses," Laura would always say after she had bought items that she definitely had no use for. Items that Paddy knew Laura would inevitably send to the charity shop.

However, Paddy did like going to the market. At the back of the building, there was a Middle Eastern-style eatery that sold the best falafel that he had ever tasted. He was happy to go with Laura if it meant he could get his falafel hit. Plus, it amused him to see how much it thrilled her to find the bits and bobs.

"Will we eat first before looking?" Laura asked.

Paddy's stomach had been growling since 10 a.m. "Sounds like a plan," he said. They ordered food and sat at one of the eatery's little green tables on matching green chairs. Paddy's leg shook slightly.

"Are you alright?" Laura asked. Her normally wavy hair was straightened, and she was wearing the flowery perfume that she only wore for special occasions.

"I've just a dose of the hunger," he said. "I haven't eaten anything all morning and, you know what I'm like with food."

Laura had a frown etched between her eyes that only appeared when she was particularly concerned. "I still can't believe that they would let Jim go like that." Laura's younger sister, Emma, had seen him that morning walking through Collins Park with a can of cider in his hand.

"It doesn't surprise me in the least," Paddy said.

"Are we mad to be out here like this? If Jim saw us."

"Jim won't do nothing with us out in a crowd. And even if he did, then he's only putting an extra lock on his cell door."

Laura sank into her seat. "But you in the shop on your own. What if he comes back?"

"He won't," Paddy said. His jaw was set, but there was still a shake in his legs.

Laura saw them jitter. "It's okay to admit that you're afraid."

"I'm not afraid of Jim. I've seen more frightening-looking pigeons."

Laura raised her eyebrows. "For a man that's not afraid, your legs are doing some shaking."

Paddy's eye felt heavy and sore. He touched his cold fingers against the swell. "I'm nervous. Not afraid, and it's nothing to do with Jim. It's your parents."

"My parents?" Laura asked, her voice high and unbelieving. "You're not afraid of my crazy ex, but my parents put the fear into you."

Their food was brought over to the table by a waitress with long brown hair and sallow skin. "First time meeting them and look at me."

"They know Jim gave you the black eye. They know you're not going around getting into fights."

Paddy ate some of his falafel before tipping it into a pot of hummus. He wasn't sure if it tasted dryer than usual or if his taste buds had been altered by the knock to the head. "It's just..." Paddy shook his head.

"Just what?" Laura asked. She had ordered a salad and was swirling it around the bowl more so than doing any eating. "What is it?"

"Do they know I did time?" Paddy's eyes met Laura's.

"They do, and I told them that stage of your life is well behind you. And how well you're doing now."

Paddy stopped himself from asking any more questions. Still, he couldn't stop the shaking in his leg. He knew it wouldn't until the dinner with Laura's parents was over.

When they had finished eating, they went looking around the stalls. Paddy thought it was just the usual sellers until they came to the cluttered stall set up in the middle of the room. The man standing behind the stall wore a green suit with a purple shirt. Paddy wasn't into fashion in the least, but the man's suit hurt his eyes.

The man seemed oblivious to the fact that he looked somewhat clownish and smiled confidently at the two. "A very happy Paddy's Day to ye both," he said. "My name is Jackser. Welcome to my bazaar." He stuck out his hand.

Laura laughed and shook the man's hand.

"Think you might be in the wrong country to have a bazaar," Paddy said. There was a large selection of items on the stall. On Paddy's quick glance, he saw boxes of tea, masquerade masks, plants, stopwatches, and little jewellery boxes.

Jackser rubbed his chin and studied Paddy. His eyes landed inconspicuously on Paddy's injury. "You're a man in need of luck."

"Did the black eye give it away?" Paddy asked.

"I think we could all use a bit of luck," Laura said.

"Some more than others," Jackser said. His hand hovered over the jewellery boxes before it dived down and retrieved a little square box. "This is the exact thing." He showed the contents to Paddy and Laura. There were two gold shamrock cufflinks inside with a green jewel in the middle of each shamrock.

"Cufflinks?" Paddy asked.

"Lucky cufflinks," Jackser said. "Luckiest cufflinks that have ever existed. No others in all the world will be able to do what these fellas can do."

"And what is it they can do?" Laura asked. She was smiling animatedly.

Jackser touched his finger on the shamrock's leaves. "Three leaves on a shamrock. Each leaf is a life. If someone were to die while wearing the cufflinks, then they'd get three more shots of life."

Paddy laughed. "Man, you can't be going around saying that. We could sue you for misleading information."

"How do you know that I'm not telling the truth?" Jackser asked. He closed the lid on the box. "If ye aren't interested in the cufflinks then." He shrugged.

"Ah, no, we are interested," Laura said. She took the box from the table and beamed when she opened it. "And they'd look great on your shirt today."

"I've never worn cufflinks in my life," Paddy said. "And I've no great desire to start doing so now."

"You can't be called Paddy and not have shamrock cufflinks. Isn't that right?" Laura asked Jackser.

"You can't," Jackser said. "It goes against everything that your name stands for. Honestly, it's a shame that you don't own a pair of them already. Or maybe it's pure luck that these will be your first."

"You're some yoke," Paddy said. "How much are these bloody cufflinks then?"

"€30," Jackser said.

"€30," Paddy repeated. "I'd get them for a fraction of the price online."

"Real gold?" Jackser queried. "And ones that give extra lives?"

"We'll get them." Laura retrieved the purse from her handbag and had her hand on a twenty when Paddy put his hand over hers.

"I'll buy the bloody things. I'm the one who's going to be wearing them." He took a fifty from his pocket and handed it to Jackser.

"Would you like a bag?" On top of the stall was a pile of black paper bags with green shamrocks on the front. Jackser gestured to them. "I had them ordered specially for the day that's in it."

"No thanks," Laura said. "Paddy's going to be wearing them now, aren't you? Sure, it's your day. It would be mad not to wear them."

"Remember each leaf is a life. When all the leaves go, then you've no extra lives left." Jackser winked.

Paddy gritted his teeth as he smiled. "I've no plans to die anytime soon."

They browsed through a few more stalls. Paddy put the box for the cufflinks in his jacket. It felt heavier than it should.

There was the sound of cheering outside, marking the

beginning of the parade. Anyone who was still inside the marketplace left. Paddy and Laura were among them.

Outside, Laura pulled up the sleeves of Paddy's coat. "Where are they?"

"In my pocket," Paddy said. "Still warm and snug in their little coffin."

"And that's where you will be too if you don't put them on," Laura laughed. "You heard what your man in there said. Keep them on and you'll be cheating death." Laura's face paled. "I shouldn't even be joking about that, sorry."

"No need to be sorry," Paddy said.

"Just after what happened with Jim," she said. "It was a wrong thing for me to joke about."

Paddy took the cufflinks out of the box. "I'll wear them if you put them on me. I'll only end up poking myself in the eye if I even attempt to put them on."

Laura put the cufflinks on Paddy's sleeve. They shone in the sun and the green emerald in the middle of the shamrock sparkled. "Now you're as dapper as anything," she said.

"And I'm cheating death in the process. Not bad for €30."

They kissed goodbye. Paddy went down Main Street, edging his way between the people who had gathered to watch the parade. He paid the parade little attention himself, but his peripheral vision caught flashes of colour.

He arrived at the shop five minutes after his lunch break had ended. Maria was waiting by the door with her coat on. "I'm going to have to rush off on you," she said. "I want to catch what's left of the parade."

"Have a good one." Paddy went into the shop and took his jacket off. The cufflinks were foreign objects on his shirt. He forgot about them on his walk down the hill. Paddy put his jacket in the stockroom and went back into the shop. It was completely empty and probably would be for the rest of the day. Most people would go to the pub.

Paddy himself wouldn't be joining in on the drinking. When he had left jail, drink was the only constant in his life until he got sober two years ago. Two years, two months, and four days. Time went fast when you were having fun. Paddy was about to tidy the books at the front of the shop when he heard his phone vibrating. He patted his trouser pockets. His phone was usually always there. Except now it wasn't. He had put it into his coat after finishing his food.

Paddy was walking to the stockroom when he heard the door slam. "Did you forget something, Maria?" Maria was always forgetting something. It was a running joke between the two of them. He only had time to register the heavy steps on the ground before he was stabbed in the back.

There was pain. Enormous and shooting. He slid to the floor. The threadbare carpet was rough on his skin. Flashes of life. Lovely, beautiful Laura. And the other girl with different-coloured eyes. Blue and brown. Sky and earth. We all fall down.

Two Leaves

Paddy stood behind the counter. His blue eyes were glazed with fear. He wanted to scream, but the sound came out as though he were gasping for breath. Paddy's hand went to his heart. It was a *thump-thump* under his shirt. His hand searched behind his back but there was no wound. Only the slightest damp patch of sweat.

He was just about to leave the counter when Angela approached with a bundle of clothes in her hands. "Jesus Christ, Paddy, what's after happening to your face?"

Paddy touched his swollen eye. "The eye. I forgot

about the eye. Is there anything on my back?" Paddy asked. He turned around.

"No?" Angela's eyebrows raised. "What were you expecting me to find?"

Paddy ignored her. He walked over to the area where he had fallen. The carpet was in need of a hoover but that was that. It must've been a dream then. Paddy touched his eye. It stung.

"Are you alright?" Angela stood behind Paddy. Her breath was heavy on his neck.

Paddy swung around. "It must've been the hit to the head," he laughed. "I just had the most vivid daydream of my life."

Angela frowned. "Have you had that checked out?" She nodded at his eye. "Head injuries can do awful damage."

"No need. It's already nothing compared to how it looked yesterday." Paddy's head spun. He had the most alarming sense of déjà vu. He saw Angela's items on the counter. Even in the heap that they were in, he knew exactly what he would find: two Aran jumpers, a Pilates DVD, and a book on gardening. When he went over to the counter, his suspicions were proven correct.

"They're nice cufflinks. What is it, a two-leaf clover?"

Paddy saw them then. One of the leaves was missing, taking with it a piece of the jewel that was in the centre of the shamrock. His stomach swirled. "Two leaves," he said.

"Must be some new take on the four-leaf clover," Angela said.

Paddy's fingers shook as he totalled Angela's items.

She watched him, her head tilted. "Are you here for the day?"

"I am." He looked at his cufflinks. Paddy put Angela's items into a paper bag and pushed them towards her. "Have a good day," he said. "Enjoy your gardening."

"How did you know that I was going to do gardening?" she asked.

"Lucky guess," Paddy said.

"I suppose it is the weather for it." Angela's phone rang inside her handbag. She rolled her eyes. "Probably work seeing if I can come in. I'll see you next week."

Paddy waved goodbye. He was about to tell her to be careful with the door, but it was too late as she let it fall behind her and the glass rattled in the pane.

"Who's banging the door?" Maria came out of the

stockroom. "One of these days that glass is going to shatter, and then we'll have a lawsuit on our hands. As well as a black eye." Maria frowned when she looked at Paddy. "Any news from the guards on that Jim fella?"

Paddy shook his head.

The door opened. Laura walked in. Her floral perfume filled the shop. She walked over to Paddy. "It looks even worse," she said before kissing him.

He held his arms out with the cufflinks facing her. "Have you seen these before?"

Laura's eyes widened. "You're wearing cufflinks?"

Paddy ran his tongue over his lips. They felt cracked and dry. "But have you seen them before?"

"No? Should I have?"

Maria, who had been hanging jumpers, came over to them. "You'd want to head off now or I won't get to see any of the parade."

"Grand," Paddy said. He took his coat from the stockroom and put it on. Outside, he took a deep gulp of air. He could hear a brass band playing. He knew they were set up on Main Street. He could see them sitting on the temporary stage with little shamrocks attached to their matching blazers.

Laura linked her arm with his. "Are you feeling alright? We don't have to go through town."

"I'm good," Paddy said. He picked up his speed. They turned onto Main Street. Just as he imagined, the brass band were there. Paddy felt dizzy.

They continued to the top of Main Street until they came to a large old building that used to be a carpet shop.

"Will we eat first before looking?" Laura asked.

Paddy's stomach growled in response. "I could definitely eat."

They ordered their food and sat on green chairs in front of a green table. Paddy's leg shook.

"Are you alright?" Laura asked.

"Do you ever get the feeling that you've experienced something before?"

"Like déjà vu?"

Paddy nodded. "It's the strangest thing, but I swear I've experienced this all before. But it could be just the…" He touched his fingers against the eye. "Probably just everything happening right now."

"Is this to do with Jim? The pulse in Laura's neck tremored. "I still can't believe that they would let him go."

"It doesn't surprise me in the least," Paddy said.

"Are we mad to be out here like this? If Jim saw us…"

"We're safe here in a crowd."

Laura sank into her seat. "But you in the shop on your own. What if he comes back?"

"He won't," Paddy said. His jaw was set and squared but there was still a shake in his legs.

Laura saw them jitter. "It's okay to admit that you're afraid."

"I'm just starving. Probably my blood sugar is getting low. Nothing to worry about." He smiled at her. But all he could see was Jim. Jim and his anger when he had stormed into the shop last night. Jim's purple face as he swung at him.

After eating, they went browsing around the stalls. Paddy did his best to manage his feeling of déjà vu as he followed Laura around the market. It would be unusual not to feel a sense of sameness when this was their usual Sunday routine. He nearly had himself convinced of this until they came to the cluttered stall in the middle of the room.

The man standing behind the table wore a green suit

and a purple shirt. His hair was dark with a few greys in the front. His eyes were electric blue.

"A very happy Paddy's Day to ye both." He stuck out his hand. "My name is Jackser. Welcome to my bazaar."

Paddy's food felt heavy in his stomach. He could see Laura shake the strange man's hand. He could hear the band playing outside. He pulled up his sleeves and looked at his cufflinks. One arm first and then the other. There was a neat assortment of jewellery boxes on the table. Paddy could remember buying the cufflinks from Jackser. *Not possible.*

Jackser's eyes were on him. "One leaf gone already," he said. "Only two left."

Paddy's hands shook. "I'm going to wait outside."

He didn't know that Laura was following him until he was out in the sunshine, and he felt her hand on his shoulder. "What was that all about?" she asked.

"I think it was just the food didn't sit right with me," Paddy said. A group of youths passed them. One of them had a bottle of Coke that looked suspiciously light in colour. The whiskey walk, Paddy used to call it. He wanted nothing more than to go to the nearest pub and find a bit of solace.

"Your man inside there, he said something about a leaf gone?" Laura asked. She was frowning deeply—a mixture of the sun in her face and utter confusion. "What was he talking about?"

"I think he must've confused me with someone else. I've one of those faces, don't I?"

"No," Laura said. "And especially not with your eye."

Cheers rang out from the bottom of the hill. "I better get back to work. Maria's raring to go to the parade."

"Alright," Laura said reluctantly. "I'll meet you straight after work."

They kissed goodbye. Paddy watched Laura walk away and then edged his way down Main Street. The day itself was mild but he was freezing and his stomach was indeed nauseous. When he was a child, he used to get delirious when he was sick. Maybe that was what was happening now. This feeling of repeating the day was just the start of a sickness. There was no other explanation.

Maria waited at the front door. Her coat was on and zipped. "I'm going to have to rush off on you. I don't want to miss what's left of the parade."

"Have a good one," he said. Paddy took his coat off and hung it up in the stockroom. He walked slowly—

anything to avoid triggering the bomb that was his stomach. He had just begun tidying the books at the front of the shop when his phone vibrated. Paddy was crossing the room when he heard the door slam. Stomps on the carpet. He turned around and only saw a flash of a thick black glove before he felt the excruciating pain in his back.

Paddy fell onto the threadbare carpet. *It wasn't déjà vu.* His eyes flickered closed. He saw lovely, beautiful Laura. He saw the other girl with different-colour eyes. And then there was nothing.

One Leaf

Paddy stood behind the counter. His back was on fire. Again, there was no blood.

A flash of gold. The cufflinks were still there, with only one leaf left. There had been three, like any other shamrock. Paddy could remember Laura attaching the cufflinks to his sleeves. Two perfect gold shamrocks with the green gem in the middle. He could remember. He wasn't crazy. *Someone wants me dead.* The thought struck him clean and clear. He was repeating the day because someone knife-hungry had killed him.

Angela left her items on the counter. "Jesus Christ, Paddy, what's after happening to your face?"

"Decked by a customer. I'm okay. No need to worry." Paddy pointed to the camera above the till. "The camera isn't working, but the fella who hit me has been arrested anyways."

"Are you alright?" Angela asked. "Did you get your eye checked?"

"To be honest, I'm not alright. I keep dying, Angela. This is the second time today. It's like I've taken a load of drugs. That or I'm going mad." He glared at Angela. "Would you say that I'm going mad?"

Angela laughed nervously.

Neither of them spoke as Paddy entered the items into the till. He put them in a paper bag and waited for her to take them. "Have a great day with your gardening."

Angela left, letting the door slam behind her. It was even more of a ferocious *bang* now. It rattled the glass loud enough that for a moment Paddy thought it would fall out. He left the counter just as Maria was storming out of the stockroom.

"It was one of the customers slamming your door. If I die again, I'll tell her not to do it. How does that sound?

Now I'll just head off on my break, so you still get to see the parade." He went and got his coat.

Maria was standing in the middle of the shop staring at him. "Am I hearing things, or did you say something about dying?"

Paddy put on his coat. "I did, didn't I? It's the lack of food. You know how I get when I haven't eaten anything."

"Well, go off then. Herself is here." Maria's eyes were on the door.

Laura opened it. She smiled before she saw the black eye. "It looks even worse," she said and kissed Paddy.

"It's no worse," he said.

They left the shop. He could hear the brass band playing. It grew louder when they turned onto Main Street.

Paddy was covered in sweat by the time they walked to the top of the hill and entered the old carpet shop.

"Will you order food for me?" Paddy asked Laura. "I just need to check something out over here." He could see the cluttered stall but was standing at the wrong angle to view the man running it.

"Are you sure you're okay?" Laura asked. Her eyes

were concerned. That little frown line was back.

"Flying it," Paddy said. "I've just got a dose of the hunger, and I don't want you seeing what I'm going to buy."

Laura was appeased. "I'll order you your usual."

Paddy waited for Laura to walk away before going over to the cluttered stall. The man, Jackser, still wore his green suit with the purple shirt underneath.

"Paddy. My favourite customer of the day returns."

"What the hell did you do to me?" Paddy asked. He lifted up a sleeve, revealing a cufflink.

"Only one life left." Jackser smiled. There was a little frame in the middle of the table that said Jackser's Bazaar. He took it up and polished its glass with a hanky that had been in his pocket.

"So how are you dying? It's happening not long after you leave here. I'm just showing a pretty redhead one of the masks and then the next thing, she's gone and the light and sounds are different. I'll get to see her again in an hour if you don't get yourself killed first."

Paddy's hand went to his back. "This isn't possible."

"It is. Very possible. Like I told you the last time I saw you, the shamrock gives you three lives. You've already exhausted two. Now, is your death something that can be prevented? Were you hit by a car or did that person who gave you the black eye come back and finish what was started?"

"Jim," Paddy said. "It had to have been Jim." Paddy's hand reached for his back once again. "I was stabbed. Both times I'm turned around and then I hear someone running at me and there's this agony and then nothing." Paddy closed his eyes.

"You know the killer and you know how it was done," Jackser said. "All you have to do is prevent it from happening again. And like the fella says, prevention is better than any cure. And you certainly weren't cured if you're missing two leaves. Just an idea, but perhaps the best thing to do in this circumstance is kill him before he can kill you. That's if you're sure it was this Jim fella. Are you sure?"

"I've no other enemies," Paddy said. "It could only be him."

"Then go off and stop him," Jackser said.

Paddy's back hurt and his heart was racing. "I don't suppose you've anything on your stall that can help me do that?"

Jackser shook his head and gave another one of his wolfish smiles. "I gave you life. Up to you to make sure it doesn't vanish."

"There you are," Laura said.

"You must be Laura," Jackser said. He stuck out his hand. "My name is Jackser. Welcome to my bazaar."

Laura laughed and shook his hand.

"I guess we better go and get our food." Paddy ushered Laura away from Jackser's stall.

"Good luck, Paddy," Jackser said. "Come back to me later and let me know how it goes."

"Good luck with what?" Laura asked.

They sat at the little green table with the green chairs and their food was brought over. "I was just telling him that the shop will be busy later. Or at least, I hope it will be busy." Paddy stared at his food.

"Did you hear a word I just said?" Laura asked.

"I'm just hungry," he said. "You know what I'm like when I haven't eaten."

"Well, why don't you eat something then instead of giving your food evils?" Laura laughed. She moved her salad around the bowl but didn't eat either.

"Did the guards ring you about Jim?" Paddy asked.

Laura swallowed her food. "No." She filled a glass of water from a jug on the table and took a drink. "Let's just go. I'm sure they'll put our food into boxes."

"Go?" he asked. "Why would we?"

"You're worried about Jim. Being out here in the open." Laura shrugged. "I hate him. I know you're not meant to hate people but fuck, I hate him."

Paddy took a bite of his falafel and then checked the time on his phone. He always took his lunch break from 12 p.m. to 1 p.m. The first time that he had died, he was five minutes late back to the shop. And the murder had happened within two minutes. 1:07 p.m. On the second time he was murdered, he had not been late back and had had time to start tidying the books but still, he judged the murder had happened at the same time. It was now 12:20 p.m. That gave him forty-seven minutes left to live, if his calculations were correct. The easiest way to prevent everything was just not to go to the shop. Or be there waiting with some form of protection to stop Jim.

What, though? What could I use to protect myself but not kill Jim? Even better, if I could record Jim stabbing the mannequin. I could set my phone down on the counter and hide it?

Paddy saw it clear in his mind. He could set up one of the mannequins at the back of the room. Put them in his own clothes and hide underneath the counter. Jim would run forward and stab the mannequin and Paddy would grab his phone and run from the shop. *And Jim runs at you as soon as he realises his mistake?* Jim wasn't in great shape. He also smoked twenty cigarettes a day. Paddy was a runner. He had quit boozing and started running instead. *I'll take the chance.* Plus, the Garda station was a five-minute walk from the shop and a two-minute run.

"Are you okay?" Laura asked. "You're off away in your own world."

"I was just thinking. I'm going to head back to the shop early. Maria's mad to see the parade, and I don't want her to be late."

"The parade isn't starting for another half an hour or so," Laura said. "And to be fair, I don't think she's missing out on much. It's always a blink-and-you-miss-it job."

"There's the chance that she'll let me leave early." He took another falafel and popped it into his mouth. *My last meal.* The thought made him queasy. He took a drink of water. "I'd prefer to be early meeting your parents than late."

Laura smiled. For a moment, she looked carefree without Jim as a shadow in her mind. Jim, who she had only dated for several months years ago but who refused to leave her alone. There would be weeks when he would vanish, but he would always return. He was tricky about it, too. He made sure to appear when Laura was on her own.

There was little the Gardaí could do without any actual proof. Yesterday's attack on Paddy had been the first of his assaults where there was evidence that Jim had been the assailant. Not that he had ever physically assaulted Laura. It was all mental.

Paddy's mind was made up. He would record Jim, and he would bring the evidence straight to the Gardaí. Maybe dying twice already would be worth it if it meant finally stopping Jim.

Ten minutes later, and Paddy was back in the shop. Maria was standing behind the counter.

"It's never one o'clock already, is it?"

"It's not," Paddy said. "But I said I'd be a dote and let

you go early. I know you're only mad to get to the parade."

Maria didn't have to be told twice. She had her coat on and was out the door, beaming at Paddy. "I'll bring you back a present," she said. And she was gone.

Paddy surveyed the empty shop. He took a deep breath. *Maybe I have finally lost the plot. The last few years of rebuilding my life have all been for nothing and I'm just pure delirious.* Yet his thoughts didn't stop him from taking one of the mannequins from the window, moving it to the back of the shop and undressing it. He brought the clothes into the stockroom and put them on himself. He scooped his clothes from the floor and dressed his stand-in.

Paddy moved to the shop's front door and inspected his work. It was pretty convincing, bar the big, bald white head. Paddy usually always wore a hat, but he hadn't bothered with one that day. As luck would have it, his usual brown woollen hat was underneath the counter. Paddy took it out and put it on the mannequin. There was still a chunk of white visible. Paddy might be on the lower end of the pale scale but he wasn't quite snow white. There was an assortment of scarves on a rail next to the coats. Paddy chose one that he found the least repulsive and then put it on the mannequin.

He stood back and surveyed once again. It would do. He checked the time on his phone. It was now five to one. Another twelve minutes.

Paddy was just setting his phone up on the counter when he caught sight of his reflection. He looked like a caricature of an Irishman in the green blazer and corduroy trousers. His hands were shaking and his heart was thumping. *This is madness.* He might be faster than Jim, but that was assuming that he could even get out the door before Jim slaughtered him. There was every chance that wouldn't happen. *And I'm on my final life.*

Paddy pocketed his phone. The keys for the shop were kept under the till. Paddy switched off the overhead light and then locked the door behind him. He rang Maria and pressed the phone to his ear. Much to his surprise, Maria answered after only two rings. "I had to close the shop. There's a problem with the electricity. I got a little shock but I'm grand. The electrician said that none of us is to go back until it's sorted. It'll probably be tomorrow."

The brass band were still going strong. Paddy could hear them clearly as he walked away from the charity shop and even louder through the phone.

"You're having all the luck, aren't you?" Maria asked. "Are you alright?" she shouted into the phone.

"I'm grand. I'm going into the Caredoc now. I better go."

"Goodbye, love. Keep me updated."

Paddy walked the opposite way he had done earlier in the day. He would go home and mull over what he would do next. At least locked in his flat he would be safe there. Safer than the charity shop anyways. Paddy picked up his pace. He turned left and took the shorter route down an alleyway made up of steep steps that were enclosed by graffiti-covered walls. The alleyway stank of cheap beer and urine. There were cigarette butts and crisp packets littering the ground. Paddy was walking past a piece of graffiti that showed a joint-smoking alien when he felt his phone vibrate. Paddy took the phone from his pocket and answered the call. It was Laura.

"He's in a coma," Laura said. "They don't think he's going to pull through."

"Who's in a coma?" Paddy asked.

"Jim. He had a seizure in the cell and whacked his head off the bars. He was lying in his own blood for ages before they even knew he was hurt."

"Jim." Paddy froze on the well-worn steps. Engines of vintage cars crawled up the hill behind him. They were always the last to join the parade. Their sound blocked out the steps running behind him. "When did this happen?"

"Last night," Laura said. "It wasn't him that Emma saw."

"Shit," Paddy said just as the knife went into his back. Pain, dark, and draining. He gazed down and saw his blood trickle on the ground. Paddy fell forwards and tumbled down the steps. His eyes were closed by the time he stopped falling. Still, he saw lovely and beautiful Laura and the other girl with different-coloured eyes.

Stem

Paddy stood behind the counter. The pain in his back was horrendous. He patted it. Surely there would have to be blood now. No one could survive being stabbed three times and not have some form of scarring.

"Three times," Paddy said. "I should be dead." He

patted his sides and then his chest. Everything was real. Everything was solid.

"Jesus Christ, Paddy. What happened to your eye?"

"My eye?" Paddy asked. *It was Jim. But Jim didn't kill me. Jim's in a coma. Then who wants me dead?*

"Just some customer," Paddy said. He looked at his cufflinks. No leaves left. Now it was just a stem. "I should be dead," he said.

"What's that?" Angela leaned in closer. She had placed a bundle of clothes on the counter. Her hands rested on top of them.

"I should be dead with the pain of my eye," he said. "Maybe you get second chances to have another shot at life. Or just to know it's your final hour."

Angela tilted her head when she looked at him. "Have you had that eye checked out?"

"No need." Paddy put Angela's shopping into a brown paper bag. "Tell you what, it's my day. I'll give you your clothes on the house."

"No, you won't," Angela said.

"You're in here supporting us the whole time, consider it a thank you."

"Very well," Angela said. She took the bag from the

counter. "If that's what you want."

"It is," Paddy said.

"Have a good day for yourself," Angela said.

"I'll try my best." Paddy watched Angela leave the shop and slam the door behind her.

"Who's banging the door?" Maria asked.

"I know," Paddy said. "One of these days the glass will fall from the door."

Maria's nod was vigorous. "And then we'll have a lawsuit on our hands as well as a black eye. Any news from the guards on that Jim fella?"

He had a seizure and now he's in a coma. "None," Paddy said. "I'm sure we'll hear something soon enough."

"Please God," Maria said.

"I'm going to head off for my lunch break now. That way I'm back with well enough time for you to see the parade."

"Off you go," Maria said.

Paddy put his coat on. The brass band was playing the Pink Panther theme song. Not a song that soundtracked St. Patrick's Day too well but it fitted Paddy's day. At least, he thought so. Laura appeared just as Paddy was set to turn onto Main Street.

"You took your lunch break early?" she asked. Then seeing his black eye added, "it looks even worse."

"It's grand," Paddy said. "It's the very least of my worries."

"What else have you to worry about?" Laura asked. "It's not Jim, is it? Has he done something else?"

"Jim isn't going to bother us," Paddy said.

"What are you worried about then?" Laura asked.

"I'm worried if I don't eat something soon then I'll fall down with the hunger." He added a smile and started walking up the hill. "This is what happens when I skip breakfast."

They arrived at the old carpet shop. Paddy gave Laura the same spiel that he had given her before and asked her to order food for him while he went over to Jackser's stall.

"Paddy is back from the dead once again," Jackser said. "How does it feel to die three times and be standing here telling the tale?"

"You said the last time that I only had one more life left? Am I a feckin' ghost now?" Paddy asked.

Jackser laughed. Sharp and loud, he laughed. "And

you did have one more life left after that life. Now after this life, you've none. Die this time and you really will be a ghost."

Paddy's back throbbed. Not someone walking on his grave but plunging on it. "You've got cufflinks that give extra lives, surely you've something on your table to help me stop my killer."

Jackser laughed again. "I'm feeling a sense of déjà vu. So, you didn't find out who killed you or couldn't you stop them?"

"It wasn't who I thought it was," Paddy said. "And now I've no idea who it is. I can't think of anyone else who'd want me dead."

Jackser shrugged. "Surely you haven't come this far in life without making more than one enemy?"

"That's the thing: Jim was the only one. At least that I'm aware of. If you could give me something that would reveal who wants me dead?"

"Nope," Jackser said. "You've got to figure that one out for yourself."

"I've got money. I could give you money."

"I can't help you," Jackser said. The smile never left his face.

"You've got to help me. I'm actually begging you, man."

Jackser smiled and crossed his arms.

Paddy stormed away. He found Laura sitting at the table. She smiled when she saw him. "Did you get what you were looking for?" she asked.

Paddy sat down and burrowed his head into his hands. "No."

"And what were you looking for? It must've been incredibly important to get you into this state."

"It is." Paddy raised his head. It felt sore and heavy. "You're the best thing that's ever happened to me. I know that's the corniest thing to say but it's true." He paused. "I didn't think life would ever be as good as it turned out."

Laura's face reddened. "What's brought all of this on?"

Paddy sighed. "When she died. When Susan died, I wanted to end it. I tried to, too. I never told you that, did I?"

Laura's eyes were misty. "No, you didn't."

"I came around in the hospital hours later. Every part of me was in shreds. I vowed then that I'd stay alive. It would be more of a punishment to live with the knowledge that I caused her death than to drift off to sleep."

"You didn't cause her death," Laura said. "We've been through this before."

"I sold her the pills." Paddy's jaw was set. "I handed her the poison."

"You didn't know they were a bad batch," Laura said.

"I won't run from the blame. I fully accept my responsibility."

The sallow-skinned server brought over their food and left it on the table. Paddy eyed his falafel. He picked it up and put it down again. "I was trying to think of people who hated me and the only solid one that I could think of was Jim." He sighed. "But plenty of people hate me."

"What's happened?" Laura asked. "Something happened."

Paddy shook his head. "I had a nightmare that I was stabbed. Think it was Jim's knock to the head. Nothing to worry about."

"Has Jim threatened you again?"

"He hasn't." For a moment, he thought of telling her that Jim was in a coma. The words were there on his tongue, but he swallowed them. Let the guards tell her the news.

Laura's shoulders relaxed but they were still too high to be comfortable. "No one hates you. Everyone around here is mad about you."

"They don't know what I did. I'm just Paddy who volunteers at the charity shop. They've no idea who I am. What I'm after doing."

"You sold drugs when you were what, nineteen? You'd no idea that there was anything wrong with them. You handed yourself into the guards then, when you found out Susan died. And then you did your time. But you're still doing time in your mind, aren't you? Every day, you're hurting yourself."

Paddy was back in the court. He remembered all the eyes on him. Susan's parents and her mass of friends. "Her parents wanted me dead. They would've killed me there and then if they could. And could you blame them?"

"Stop it," Laura said. She held Paddy's hands. "Stop hurting yourself."

Paddy did his best to nod. He changed the subject. If this was to be their last conversation, then he didn't want Laura remembering him as a pitiful mess. They talked about dinner that evening and the summer that was forever just around the corner. When it was time to go, Paddy kissed her, hoping it wouldn't be the last time.

At the charity shop, Maria waited at the door. "I'm going to have to rush off on you," she said. "I want to catch what's left of the parade."

"Have a good one," Paddy said. "Have the best one."

When she left, he took the keys for the shop out from underneath the counter, and he locked the front door. Once that was done, he inspected the shop. There was no one there but of course, there wouldn't be. His attacker had banged the door when entering the shop. After Paddy's quick inspection, his phone vibrated in his pocket. A few heartbeats later and the hand rattled the door.

Paddy was at the back of the shop. But he could see Angela clearly enough. Their eyes locked—the same green eyes that had glared at him in the courtroom all those years ago. She had looked different then, with an extra five stone and long, dark hair.

Paddy walked across the room. The floorboards creaked underneath his feet.

He unlocked the door and opened it. Angela had on her

gardening gloves. "You're Susan's mam," he said.

Angela stepped in through the open door. "I am." Her green eyes were searching. "When did you figure out who I was, or did you always know? Could you pretend that Angela was my real name as easily as I could?"

"I only just figured it out." Paddy spotted the glint of silver behind her back. "You're the only person who'd have justifiable reason to kill me. That's what you're here to do, isn't it?"

Angela's normally friendly face had vanished, replaced with one that wanted to bite. "You shouldn't live when she's gone."

"I tell myself that every day," Paddy said.

"Oh, I know. I heard all about your guilt from the AA meetings. You're mad to spill the beans there. Next thing, you'll be writing a book, talking about your big bad grief and all the terrible things it's been doing to you. You spill your soul out, not thinking that there could be someone there who knew Susan. Not one of my friends who brought everything back to me. You and your big mouth. Happy to tell each and every person that you were volunteering your way into forgiveness. Being the hero while my daughter rots in her coffin."

"I'm sorry," Paddy said. "I truly am sorry."

Angela rolled her eyes. "You never told who gave you the pills. You kept your mouth shut on that one. Even when you could've reduced your time, you were silent. Another heroic move from my child's killer. Her father's killer, too. Did you know that? They said it was a heart attack, but I know it was the pain of losing our daughter."

"I am sorry," Paddy said. He was crying now.

"You go about your life, laughing at everything. But you're still just as much scum as you ever were, aren't you?" Angela's eyes were venomous. "Terrorising poor Laura. You must think I'm some idiot, telling me that a customer did that to you." Her eyes landed on the black eye. "It was a pity her new fella didn't kill you."

"Her new fella?" Paddy asked. He rubbed his head. "I am her new partner. It's Jim who decked me. He's been terrorizing her since she broke up with him." His phone was still vibrating in his pocket. Laura's name was on the screen, accompanied by a picture of the two of them taken at New Year's. He flashed the phone at Angela. "She's ringing me now."

"To tell you to stay away," Angela said but doubt was evident in her voice.

"Do you want to speak with her?"

"I do."

Paddy answered the phone and pressed it to his ear. Laura told him that Jim was in a coma. "I hope he'll be alright," Paddy said and he meant it—despite all that Jim had done he still wouldn't wish death on him. "I have someone here in the shop with me. She wants to talk to you for a second." Paddy passed the phone to Angela.

It was a short call. When it ended, Angela handed the phone back to Paddy.

"She'd be heartbroken if anything happened to you, I suppose."

"She would," Paddy said. "More than I can imagine. She loves me more than I deserve. Way more than I deserve."

"Susan was all about peace and love for everyone. She wouldn't've blamed you. She didn't hold grudges. I tried not to hate you. I tried to be like her. When I found out you worked here, I used to come and keep an eye on you. Just to make sure you were behaving." Angela closed her eyes, igniting deep wrinkles around the sides. "This morning, I was getting petrol, and I heard women talking about Laura. About how she had been tormented by her ex, who worked in the charity shop and how her new fella had given him a black eye and a warning to stay away." Angela dropped the knife from her hands. She jumped when it hit the ground. "I was so close to killing you, Paddy." Her hands were shaking, worse than Paddy's had ever done with the DTs. "I would've killed you." Her eyes were frightened and searching. "I thought you were after hurting not just my Susan but Laura, too."

She rubbed her hands on her trousers. "I won't…" She stepped away from the knife and towards the door. "I won't come back anymore." She turned the key in the lock and held the door open.

"I'm sorry for…" She glanced at the knife. "I'm so very sorry."

"I'm sorry too," Paddy said.

Angela pulled off her gardening gloves and slipped them into her handbag. Then she was gone, leaving Paddy staring at the door. His eyes lowered to the knife on the ground. He picked it up, wrapped it in a scarf and put it behind the counter.

Paddy's hands tingled. He opened the front door and inhaled the cold spring air. The brass band was still playing. He knew the tune but couldn't remember what it was called. It beat its rhythm onto his heart.

The End

JACK-IN-THE-BOX

Jack left the milking parlour and went into the cold morning. It was giving good weather for the afternoon, but it was hard to imagine that manifesting with the cut of the sky. Jack's boots made a squelching sound in the mud as he walked towards the old farmhouse. Uncle Pierce, the man visible through the dirty kitchen window, was one of a long line born in the farmhouse. Jack could see the top of the grey head as Pierce piled logs into the stove.

Jack pushed the latch on the blue door, and he entered the porch. The walls were covered in peeling yellow paint. On the worn linoleum floor were muddy boots and spent runners. Another door later, and Jack entered the stiflingly warm kitchen. A large kitchen table stood centre in the room. To the left of the kitchen was a dresser with an assortment of delph; next to the dresser was a large wood-burning stove. At the opposite end sat a white Aga grey with dirt. On either side of the Aga were the cupboards and worktop.

Pierce was bent before a large wood-burning stove, throwing logs onto the fire. He had on his good red jumper that was usually kept for Christmas. "Took you long enough with the milking."

"Good morning to you, too," Jack said.

"It is a good morning for me." Pierce's voice was deep, smoky, and he constantly sounded like he was on the verge of coughing.

"Not like you to have the kitchen so warm," Jack said. Normally, the stove wouldn't be lit until later in the day, and when it was, there'd only be a few logs used.

"Take off your fecking boots." Pierce threw one more log into the fire and stood up as straight as his stooped back would allow him. He was just past sixty, but a lifetime of poor diet and hard work had left him looking twenty years older.

Jack had left a trail of mud behind him. Just as well, he had only taken a few steps. If he did that at home, his wife, Aoife, would scald him, but normally Pierce wouldn't even notice. Not that Jack would usually leave his boots on, but a bad night's sleep had left him with brain fog. "Sorry about that," Jack said. He went to the porch and took off the boots.

There was a hole in his sock, and a toe jutted out of the coarse material. When he went back into the kitchen, Pierce was smoking one of his rollies. Already, the tip of the cigarette was damp.

"You can clean the floor up after you," Pierce said. "I spent half the morning getting it to this level."

"You cleaned the floor?" Jack asked. He didn't even try to mute the disbelief in his voice. Pierce was no cleaner. Once a week, Nuala Finnerty used to come in and clean the house, but that ceased when she had broken her hip at the beginning of autumn.

"I did," Pierce said. He held an ashtray in his hand and tapped the ash into the clean glass. He took a few nervous pulls on the cigarette and nubbed it out. He set the ashtray on top of the kitchen table and checked his reflection in the mirror above the stove. There was a tiny piece of toilet paper on his cheek, with a speck of red on the white.

While Pierce inspected himself, Jack looked around

the room. It wasn't sparkling but it was clean. Gone were the piles of papers and laundry from the kitchen table. Gone was the mound of dirty dishes from the sink and worktop. Everything was wiped down and in neat order.

"You didn't do all this, did you?" Jack asked.

"Well it wasn't the tooth fairy," Pierce said. He strolled past Jack and went to the kettle and flicked the switch on. "You'll have a cup of tea with me." He kept his back turned as he took two mugs out of the highest cupboard.

"I better get back to herself. We're heading off to Enniscorthy later. There's some craft fair she wants to visit. You wouldn't think she'd have an interest in that sort of thing, would you? But there's some woman selling jewellery there that has a bit of a following on Instagram."

"Aoife will be half the day getting ready. You've plenty of time to sit and have tea with me. We should be having something stronger."

Jack knew that Pierce was right. He just wasn't in the mood to get words from his uncle. Yet if he only wanted to give out, then he wouldn't be going to the trouble of making tea. "Why is it we should be having something stronger?"

"I've a bit of news to tell you." Pierce took two teabags from the box of Lyon's on the worktop and put them into the chipped cups.

"What kind of news?" Jack asked.

Pierce glanced over his shoulder and smiled. "I'm not dying, if that's what you were hoping."

"Course, I wasn't hoping that," Jack said. Even with the heat of the kitchen, the tiled floor was cold on Jack's stockinged feet. He pulled his sock out and buried his toe in the fabric. Seeing he wasn't getting home without drinking a cup of tea, Jack took the litre of milk from the fridge and lined it next to the cups.

The kettle came to a boil, and Pierce poured the water over the teabags. They shovelled sugar into their tea and then added milk. With steaming mugs, they sat before the table.

Jack noted Pierce's hair had been cut. Not by his hand, which his uncle was accustomed to doing, but by a barber, if the neatness of the cut was anything to go by.

"It's a grand cup of tea," Jack said.

"It is." Pierce rubbed his chin. "She doesn't drink tea. I've never met a person who doesn't drink tea."

"Who doesn't drink tea?" Jack asked.

"Mimi," Pierce said. "She only drinks water. I said to her, do you only eat bread then? Imagine, she'd cost me a pittance to feed."

"Who's Mimi?" Jack asked. A slap across the face, and he got it. The improvement in Pierce's appearance and the cleanliness of the house. "You've met someone?"

"Online." Pierce drank his tea. His lips smacked against the cup. "That phone you got me for Christmas turned out to be handy. I thought it would be a useless piece of junk, but I was wrong." The phone had been left in the box for weeks after Christmas before Jack had come into the house one day at the end of January to find Pierce's haggard face lit up by the phone's glow.

"Online?" Jack laughed. "You're a man of the times now. Didn't even think you'd have an interest in online dating."

"Did you think I was happy with only the cows here to keep me company?" Pierce took the phone from his trouser pocket and polished the screen with his sleeve cuff.

"I thought you were," Jack admitted. "When am I getting to meet this Mimi?"

"She's coming next week," Pierce said. "I said I'd get the house in order and get it aired out." He nodded at the stove. "Get a good bit of heat into the place and get rid of the damp."

"Next week," Jack said. "Where is it she's coming from?"

"Thailand. She'll come over for the month, and we'll get to know each other better. All going well, we'll tie the knot in the summer."

"Married?" Jack spat out his tea over the clean table. "Jesus, I'm sorry about that." He looked in the cupboard under the sink and found a new pack of cloths. He took one out, wet it and cleaned the table. "You're thinking of getting married." Jack sat down with the cloth still in his hand. He held it tightly in his fist. "This isn't one of your jokes, is it?"

"Why would you think the idea of me getting married to be such a joke?" Pierce didn't frown, nor did he crack a smile. He only sat there, drinking his tea.

"I don't." Jack smiled half-heartedly. "But you've never even mentioned this Mimi one, and the next thing, you're telling me the two of ye are going to get married."

"As long as we get along okay when she visits. I can't

see why we won't. We're talking the whole time, and we get along rightly then."

"But married?" Jack said. "That's a huge step, isn't it?"

"I didn't say nothing when you told me you were marrying herself. Speaking of which, you should get back to her. You've drank your tea and heard my news. You'll be here tomorrow and you can tell me you're happy for me then."

Jack looked at his tea. There was more than half left. He took it over to the sink and poured it in. Normally, liquid was slow going down the drain, but Pierce must've declogged it. When Jack turned around, Pierce was on his phone with a smile on his face. "You know, I am happy for you. It was just a bit of a shock is all." He waited for Pierce to say something, but he didn't say a word. "I'll see you tomorrow," Jack said. He went into the porch, and as he put on his boots, he could hear Pierce laughing. It was a sound Jack wasn't used to hearing. It didn't sound right.

Jack walked across the yard to his decades-old hatchback. It was black but it was so covered in mud, you'd think it was brown. They wouldn't be going to

Enniscorthy in his car, that was for sure. It had been years since Aoife had gone anywhere in it. Not that he'd blame her. The inside was clean enough, but the seats were taped together in places, and there was an odd smell that air fresheners couldn't disguise. It was the most un-Aoife car that there could be. She hated Jack driving it. She'd asked him over and over to get rid of it, but the truth of the matter was that they couldn't afford to replace it. Aoife's fancy Sportage already stretched them as it was.

Jack got into his car. There were a few drops of rain on the screen. He turned on the wipers and watched them disappear. Imagine, Pierce Mulcahy getting married. He'd never even heard his uncle talking about women—not in the romantic sense anyway. Aoife he'd talk about; never in a good way. Aoife would probably faint when she heard the news. That, or call Jack a liar.

He was no liar. Even on those odd times when he'd tell her a white lie, she'd see right through him. Aoife, on the other hand, could maintain her poker face in any situation to the point where it was impossible to know if she was telling the truth. Jack slid the key into the ignition. Despite the battered interior and exterior, the engine sang beautifully. If she kept singing so sweetly, he'd keep her.

Jack drove through the early morning. Quiet was the road. Trees, much like those surrounding the farm, were without leaves. The winter had been a cruel one, and spring was late in coming. Sometimes it felt as though winter would stay forever. There wasn't even a peep from the daffodils yet. Normally, they'd be lining the road to Jack and Aoife's cottage. Nothing there now but frosted-over grass. The cottage itself was only two kilometres from the farm. Aoife hated living in the sticks and would have preferred to live in Enniscorthy itself. In the end, she had agreed. Not only would it make Jack's multiple daily trips to the farm easier, but one day they'd be living in the farmhouse, so she better get used to the countryside. Also, a mortgage in the beyond was much more affordable than living in town.

Coming up to their cottage, Jack could see Aoife's shiny new car in the driveway. He'd told her not to buy a white car, saying that it would only get filthy living out here. Yet she kept it dazzling. Jack parked his car a few feet away from Aoife's and got out.

No one had lived in their cottage in over a decade when they bought it. Despite dampness and an asbestos roof on the shed in the garden, the place was in good condition. A makeover and an extension later, it was a home. Here in the cold day, its green façade gave colour to the frosted-over land. There was a scattering of pink pots outside the front door, all waiting for that coveted yellow spring flower.

Much like the farmhouse, there was a porch before stepping into the main house. Their porch had white walls and pictures of Aoife and Jack staring at any would-be visitors. On the floor were blue tiles that made Jack think of the ocean. Not something he cared to think about when he had a fear of deep water.

Jack took off his muddy boots and changed into the orange slippers that Aoife had bought him for Christmas. He hadn't the heart to tell her he wasn't a fan of the colour orange.

Inside the cottage, it was sleek, with mirrors everywhere. Too many mirrors in Jack's opinion. There were only so many times a day he wanted to see his reflection. The gold mirror ahead of him showed a tall pasty man with bright blue eyes and sharp cheekbones. He wore a faded blue jumper and his old jeans.

"You're back early," Aoife said. She strolled down the hallway. Her body was hugged by a pink dressing gown, and her hair was wrapped in a pink microfiber towel. Her skin was cream fresh, and her brown eyes were free from worries.

"I'm back later than usual, actually," Jack said.

Aoife walked past him into the kitchen. Despite the extension, it was smaller than the kitchen in the farmhouse. To the right were the cupboards. A black coffee machine and kettle sat on top of the white worktop. Straight ahead was the island. Beyond the island, at the back of the room, was the Aga that had only been used a handful of times. To the left of the room, next to the window, was the kitchen table and velvet chairs.

"Coffee?" Aoife asked. "Or maybe you might want to have a shower first?"

"Do I look that bad?" Jack asked.

"You smell that bad, too," Aoife said. "More cow than man." Aoife's full lips curved into a smile.

"Well, it'll have to wait until I tell you the news."

"News?" Aoife said. "What news is this?" Her journey for coffee forgotten, Aoife turned and faced him. "Is it good news or bad?"

Jack laughed. Aoife had always been hungry for information. Working at the beauticians meant she could feed on it. "Make me a cup of coffee and I might tell you."

"Seriously? Would you not just tell me now?" Aoife grasped his jumper sleeve before dropping her hold. The material of that particular jumper was coarse and felt like sandpaper grating on her bones.

"I'm wrecked tired. Sure, I need a bit of caffeine to tell you."

Aoife rolled her eyes but made him coffee, nevertheless. When the two of them were seated at the kitchen table, he told her the news. Outside, spits of rain fell onto the glass.

"You're telling me that Pierce has ordered himself a mail-order bride?" Aoife asked. Her almond-shaped eyes weren't particularly large, but at that moment, they looked humongous.

"If you want to put it like that," Jack laughed.

"What on earth do you find funny about it?" Aoife asked. She set the mug that had been cradled in her hands onto the table. "You do realise what this means?"

"Mimi is in for an awful shock when she sees the cut of Pierce waiting for her at the airport. She'll probably get on the return flight to Thailand." The heat was on in their cottage. Jack could hear the boiler humming. Even if it was silent, you'd know it was on, for the cottage was roasting with the sheer amount of insulation that had gone into it during the renovation.

"Mimi is about to marry a very rich man who will give her a visa. With the way he looks after himself, she won't have to stay married to him for long. Then what happens? Mimi becomes a rich widow, and your rightful inheritance, your family farm, your birthright, will go to her." Aoife folded her arms. "Tell me what's funny about that, Jack?"

"Pierce wouldn't do that," Jack said. "He'd never."

"He treats you like less than a dog. Sure, you'd be nicer to a dog than what he is to you."

"He's not the worst."

Aoife smiled at him. She picked up her cup of tea from the table. She had just done her nails. They were knife-sharp and a funny brown colour that looked like dried blood. "I hope your faith in him is deserved. Otherwise, you've been slaving away for nothing."

"He pays me, doesn't he?" Jack said. "Anyway, I thought you'd be only delighted with a wedding to attend."

"Ah yeah, sure. I'll be the maid of honour." Aoife rolled her eyes. "If I knew the bad news you were going to tell me, I'd have added something stronger to the coffee. Then again, maybe I wouldn't. It's too tasty to be ruining it. It's good, isn't it?"

Jack leaned into the chair, happy to be away from the topic. "It is nice."

"Toby gave me the beans from his friend's café."

Jack almost spat out his drink again. "You and Toby are getting awful good friends, aren't ye?"

"Well, he's in doing the deliveries just about every day. Be strange if I didn't get to know him, wouldn't it? We all know him."

"I see plenty of people around here, and I don't even know their names, never mind what type of coffee they drink."

"That's cause you're unsociable. It's a wonder the two of us ever got talking in the first place."

"Well, I better get my unsociable self into the shower now that I've told you my good news." Jack poured his coffee into the gleaming sink and put the cup into the dishwasher.

"What a waste of a perfectly good cup of coffee,"

Aoife said.

"It left a funny taste in my mouth. The delivery boy wouldn't know a good cup of coffee if it hit him."

Aoife laughed. "Coming from the fella who adores instant."

Jack saw Aoife take the phone from her dressing gown pocket. Whatever she saw made her laugh. She had a great laugh. It was one you'd want to join in with. It echoed around their cottage. Jack could hear it as he got into the shower.

When he got out of the shower, Aoife was dressed in jeans and one of her soft jumpers. She had dried and straightened her hair. She smiled when she saw Jack. "There you are. You got lost in the shower, did you? Normally, you're in and out in a few minutes."

"I couldn't stop thinking about what you said," Jack said. "You don't think he wouldn't leave me the farm, do you?"

Aoife placed her palm on the top of Jack's back. "Pierce is the kindest, most thoughtful man I've ever met. I'm sure he'd do no such thing. Now, are we going to go for breakfast?" Aoife's coat, knee-length and grey, was hung on the back of the kitchen door. She took it off the hook and put it on. Jack watched her, knowing if he was to dare leave any of his coats on the door, she'd scold him before putting it out with the rest of the coats in the utility.

"We're going for breakfast?" Jack asked. "I thought we were eating here?" The kitchen that Aoife had insisted on buying had been the most expensive in the shop. She had justified the splurge by saying the two of them would cook at home and save a fortune instead of constantly eating out. Yet the kitchen had barely been used.

"We've nothing in the fridge to be eating here," Aoife said. "Now, are you ready?"

Jack put on his green parka and followed Aoife out to her car. She was sitting in the passenger's seat, inspecting her nails. The keys were waiting for Jack on the seat.

Jack put the keys into the ignition. It barely made a peep when it came on. You'd hardly think there was any power in the engine, but they were moving away from the cottage until they turned left, and there was only road behind them.

They went to a newly opened café in the middle of

Enniscorthy. Since it had opened, Aoife had been one of their frequent customers. She loved it, not only because it was a few doors away from the beautician's where she worked, but because its interior was done in the white and gold scheme she adored. Having decent food helped too. Not that Aoife ate much of anything she ordered. Out of the large fry, she had only eaten half a piece of toast, a sausage, and an egg. Jack, despite his skinny frame, ate his large breakfast and what she had left behind. While he had been eating, his mind was blissfully empty, but now the food was gone, his worries were back. "There'd have to be some sort of a law preventing him from leaving anyone else the farm. Wouldn't there?"

"We could talk to Liza on Monday?" Liza, Aoife's solicitor aunt, was handy to get advice from, as long as you didn't mind getting a barrage of snide comments. Aoife's eyes were on the window. It was a quiet morning out there but there were still a few people passing. A mischievous glint Jack hadn't seen in Aoife's eyes in a long time appeared. "Or we could sabotage their time together. That could be fun."

"How do we go about sabotaging it?"

Aoife laughed. "I was only joking. We'll ask my aunt.

Are you ready to go, or will you vomit all that food out if you try and walk?"

"I'll be fine."

It was Aoife's turn to pay. Jack waited for her outside. At the end of the hill, he could see the Tricolour flag on top of Enniscorthy Castle. They had gone there on their first date. Aoife was mad about the film Brooklyn—she'd never read the book. Despite living in Enniscorthy all her life, she hadn't been to the castle since she was ten on a school tour. Jack had insisted they visit it. Aoife had loved the Brooklyn exhibition and brought Jack to her flat to watch the movie.

Aoife came out of the café. There was a silver hat on her head now that hadn't been there earlier. She was always fishing things out of that oversized pink handbag. Jack often thought she must keep his heart around in there. "It's cold, isn't it?" Aoife asked.

"Freezing," Jack agreed. "At least the rain has stopped. Don't suppose you want to warm up with a walk to the top of Vinegar Hill?"

"I don't," Aoife laughed. "Would you be well? I want to visit this craft market and get myself a new pair of earrings from Sherry Shines."

"Sherry Shines," Jack laughed. "She sounds like a fecking porn star. She'll probably give you a link to her OnlyFans, too."

Aoife sighed. "Only you'd think like that."

They crossed the road and walked to the Poorhouse Arts Centre. Aoife told him about Sherry Shines and how she had turned her life around with her jewellery. She sold it all online but liked to attend craft fairs as a way to meet her loyal fanbase. Jack had heard it all before. Aoife had a bit of a goldfish memory; it was one of the traits that he wasn't besotted with. "She's distantly related to Toby. He said she's amazing in real life, too."

"Toby, the delivery driver?" Jack asked.

"How many Tobys do you think I know?" Aoife asked.

They walked up the short driveway to the Poorhouse Arts Centre. There was a decent-sized green to the side, with three children running around. In the middle of the green was an oak tree with a selection of colourful fairy doors stuck on its bark. A child wearing a bright yellow coat ran over to the tree and wrapped her arms around it. Ahead of them, the two-storey building was too modern for Jack's tastes but just right for Aoife's.

"Funny us going to the poorhouse before Pierce has even knocked me off the will."

"Will you ever stop?" Aoife said.

"What did I do?" Jack asked.

"Let me enjoy meeting Sherry without you talking about money. You're always worrying about money. Would you ever just enjoy yourself?" Aoife stormed ahead of him. Jack let her go, knowing that she'd need some retail therapy to burn off her anger. What she had said was true, but it was hard not to worry about money with the way she spent it.

Jack walked towards the building. He could see his reflection in the shiny glass doors. With his hands in his pockets and slow, begrudging steps, he looked only delighted with himself. He pulled the door open and a whoosh of warm air hit his face. He mightn't be ecstatic going to the craft fair, but it was good to get out of the cold. Above was a glass ceiling showing the clouds passing overhead. As Jack glanced upwards, a bird flew past, leaving a souvenir of its being on the already dirty glass. He made a mental note to say that to Aoife if she started talking about a glass conservatory. At the back of the foyer was a tiny café with a handful of chairs in front of it. Jack debated ordering a cup of something and sitting there waiting for Aoife but decided against it. It might only cost a couple of euros, but the way things were going, he'd be better keeping it in his pocket. He'd have to have a good chat with Aoife, another one, about all this spending. There was a noticeboard on the wall next to the door that led to the fair. Jack had a quick look at it. There was a poster advertising a production of *The Playboy of the Western World* by the Carnival Players and a variety of flyers for classes held in the building. None of them interested Jack. Still, he read them over and over. Only when he had almost memorised the lines did he go inside.

His eyes automatically found Aoife. She was talking to a bossy-looking woman with a sleek blonde bob and a sharp pink suit. Aoife already had a pink bag that said *Sherry Shines* but she wasn't finished shopping, judging by how she stared lovingly at the jewellery on the table. Jack knew if he went over and interrupted the conversation, he'd be in the doghouse for days.

"She's a fan of spending money," said a voice. Jack turned around. The man the voice belonged to wore a purple suit that was far too garish for Jack's tastes.

"Not a fan of the suit?" the man asked. "Sure, you

can't win them all."

Jack wasn't sure what to say so he said nothing. Instead, he looked at the man's stall. None of it looked like crafts, except maybe the odd-looking tea. The rest of it was the type of junk you'd hide away for years before throwing out in the skip. Jack believed that was where the man must've got all his *crafts*.

"You're not a fan of shopping?" the man asked.

"You one of them psychics, are you?" Jack asked. On the table was a dark red box with intricate gold swirls on it. Jack touched it.

The man laughed. Deep and throaty. He had a wide smile when it was ignited. "My name is Jackser. Welcome to my bazaar. I see you're a fan of the Jack-in-the-Box."

Jack saw the gold handle at the side of the box. "I always wanted one of these when I was a young fella. Thought they were cool, with my name being Jack."

"Isn't that funny?" Jackser said.

"You said your name was Jackser?" Jack asked.

"It is indeed. Jackser O'Keefe. It's a good name, isn't it?"

"I'm surprised you don't call yourself Jack. That's a

better name." Jack glanced at Aoife. She was always giving out to him about how unsocial he was, but here he was, talking away to a stranger.

"Well, we couldn't have three Jacks gathered at my stall now, could we?" Jackser asked.

Jack's attention was back on the Jack-in-the-Box. He stroked the top of the box. It looked like those antique toys Aoife had been temporarily fascinated with. Dragged him around to antique shows for six solid months before it became "boring and childish." With her fascination gone, everything had been sent to the attic to rot. "Does that work?" Jack asked.

"Oh, it does," Jackser said. He rolled up his sleeve, revealing the Jester tattoo on his forearm. "Would you like to have a go at it?"

"If that's alright?" Jack asked.

"Course, it's alright, Jacky Boy. It can't just sit there being idle, now, can it?"

No one had called Jack that since his grandfather Tommy had passed away twenty years ago. Hearing it there on the strangely suited man gave Jack the feeling of dipping his hand into a bucket of cobwebs. Jack picked up the box and turned the lever. It was warm, not cold, like he had expected it to be. For one strange second, he thought he felt it pulse in his hand.

Jack looked at the stallholder and saw blue eyes watching him and a nod of the head. "Go on, Jacky Boy. No need to be frightened."

"I'm not frightened," Jack said. Maybe if he bought Aoife every piece of jewellery on the stall behind him, she'd teach him her poker face. A turn of the handle and the first notes of "Pop Goes the Weasel" played. Out of his peripheral vision, Jack could see Jackser swaying from side to side. His flow sped up the faster Jack turned the lever. A child, still toddling, wandered over to the stall. His little pudgy hands clapped to the music. As soon as the lid lifted from the top of the box, revealing the red and gold-clothed Jester, with a white face, black eyes and lips, the child bawled. His mother, browsing through the neighbouring stall selling knitwear, scooped him up and walked away.

"Jesus," Jack said.

"Nothing like Jesus," Jackser said. "Completely wrong skin tone to start with."

"This isn't a child's toy, is it?" The Jester was still moving side-to-side, just like the stallholder had done seconds before.

"I wouldn't let a child anywhere near it," Jackser said. "It's no toy," he added in a whisper.

"It's an antique then," Jack said. "The Victorians sure had weird taste in toys, didn't they? Herself over there had a Victorian doll, and it used to scare me every bloody night."

"I couldn't tell you how old it is," Jackser said. "It very well might be Victorian, but I'd reckon on it being even older than that. That's not the reason I wouldn't allow a child to play with it."

"Some sort of weird paint on it, is there?" Jack could hear Aoife laughing behind him. He looked over his shoulder. She was still talking to the bossy-looking woman, but she had taken off her silver hat, and flyaway hairs stood on end, reaching for the ceiling. If she had known her hair looked like that, her hat would be back on her head.

"The paint is perfectly fine," Jackser said.

The Jester was still now, but its eyes were staring. Jack put the lid down, and the box was beautiful once again. "What's wrong with it then?" Jack asked.

"If I tell you, will you keep it to yourself?" Jackser

whispered.

"I will," Jack said. The only two people he spoke with regularly would have no interest. They'd only zone off or change the subject.

"If someone were to have a go at that box when the moon is full, when little Jack comes out of the box, it would cause them to die of fright. A very handy toy if there's someone you want to get rid of without evidence of your wrongdoing."

Jack laughed. Aoife turned around. It had been months since she had heard Jack laugh like that. That time it, had only been possible because he went picking mushrooms and had chosen the magic variety by mistake. "You're some chancer. You can't be going saying things like that or you'd get sued for fraud. Sure, you know what people are like now."

"A chancer I may be, but I'm no liar. It's the best way to get rid of someone—so I've heard anyway. Not that I've used it myself. Just saying now that there was someone you needed to get rid of then it would only work on the person turning the lever. You'd be perfectly fine if you were sitting in the room with them, then it wouldn't affect you. And it wouldn't affect them straight away.

Sure, they'd be scared but it would take an hour before the fright would get to their heart and crush it."

Jack took a step closer to the stall. He had had every intention of taking a step away, but there he was, near enough to Jackser that he could smell the faint aroma of cloves coming from him. With the lid on the box, it was beautiful once again. The man in front of him was a better liar than even Aoife but still, he could remember his upset each Christmas and birthday when his Jack-in-the-Box never came. "How much would you charge for something like this?"

"For you," Jackser said, tilting his head to the side, "and because I know money's tight in these threatening times, I'll say fifty euros."

"Fifty euro," Jack repeated. It wasn't a fortune. It was really only two dinners in one of Aoife's restaurants and she had spent three times as much on one of her discarded toys, but still: the most expensive thing Jack owned was a pair of Levi's. "What about forty?"

Jack rubbed his chin. "I might be a foolish man but forty will do me." He held out his hand to shake on the deal; Jack shook it. With the deal sealed, Jack took his battered wallet from his pocket, retrieved two crumpled twenties, and handed them to Jackser.

"Remember, the full moon is tomorrow," Jackser said.

Jack did what Aoife called his "bemused snort" and left the stall. Aoife, who had two more pink bags in her hands, was ready to leave too. They left the hall and walked out into the foyer and then out of the building. Jack held the box closer to his chest. "Not like you to stay for such a short amount of time," he said.

Aoife touched Jack's elbow. "You know when people say, never meet your heroes? Well, it couldn't be said about her. She was amazing. I'll have to tell Toby."

Jack gritted his teeth. Maybe if the Jack-in-the-Box did what Jackser said, he'd have to find Toby tomorrow. He laughed at the thought of him waiting outside the beautician's with the box in his hands.

"What's so funny?" Aoife asked. "You haven't been eating the wrong type of mushrooms again, have you?"

"Just something silly," he said. "It doesn't matter." Jack itched his nose. "Are you happy with everything you bought?"

"You're not going to give out to me for spending?" Aoife shook the bags. "There's a couple of hundred euros here, but I promise this will be it for a while."

"Alright," Jack said. It would be fine. The farm would go to him. All of it would. They'd sell their little cottage for a tidy profit, and they wouldn't have to worry about money. There was no hope Pierce wouldn't leave him the farm. No use in fighting with Aoife now, not when he had spent forty euros on a child's toy. Oh no, not a child's toy; a killer's toy.

Aoife didn't notice Jack's purchase until they were almost back at the car. "What's in that? Not a birthday present for me, is it?"

Jack did his snort laugh and said no more. It was easier that way. Maybe silence was the easiest type of lie.

***

The next morning, after Jack had finished milking, he walked over to the farmhouse. There was no threat of rain in the day now, with the sky clear of clouds. Having it so clear left it icy and the puddles were miniature icing rinks. When Jack was a child, he had loved those icy puddles and would break through them with his wellies. He would've done it there, only Uncle Pierce was staring at him through the kitchen window. They had been cleaned since yesterday. They were by no means glistening, but they were a far cut better than what they'd been the day before. Jack didn't forget about taking off his boots. This time, when he walked into the kitchen, there was a hole in both his socks.

Pierce had on a navy jumper today, one that Jack hadn't seen before, and his hair was slicked back with gel. "You were the cut of your father walking in there. I thought for a minute I was seeing a ghost."

"Yeah?" Jack asked. His father, Mick, had died twenty years before. Unlike Pierce or Jack, Mick had no interest in farming. This was why Pierce was willed the farm while Mick got the cash; money that he had quickly burned his way through. "I'm not sure if that's a compliment or not," Jack said.

"I'm not sure of that myself," Pierce said. He coughed into his elbow, a great hacking thing, but it didn't prevent him from relighting the half-smoked cigarette in the ashtray. "Do you think one day, you'll take to the drink and the women and burn your way through everything?"

"I have Aoife," Jack said. "There's no need for other women. And the drink I can leave or take." Inside the kitchen, it was stiflingly warm again. It was even cleaner now today. Pierce had washed all the cabinets; you could tell that with the cloth marks on the wood. He had also taken his late mother's favourite china set from storage and placed it on the dresser.

"Your father was forty before he went mad on the drink. The same thing could happen to you." Pierce took two sharp pulls and stubbed out his cigarette. "I'm going to get one of them vapes. I'll need to get off these bloody things before Mimi gets here. She hates smoking. Her mother died of lung cancer."

"You're serious about this Mimi woman, then." Jack saw the new kettle on the worktop. The one Pierce had had for years was dumped for this new shiny one. It was probably even one of those Bluetooth kettles that Aoife was wanting. "Do you want a cup of tea? I'll make it for you since you made me one yesterday."

"Go home to Aoife. Sure, you can't, can you? She's at the job making eyes with everyone. Being the right loyal wife." Pierce laughed. His phone beeped on the table. He picked it up and smiled at whatever he saw.

"You will leave me in your will, won't you?" Jack asked. Not what he had meant to say. Aoife had rung up her aunt last night and they were due to speak with her on Friday about Jack's rights. This outburst was not part of the plan. "If you and this Mimi one do end up married, you'd never leave her the farm, would you? She might end up being your wife but my blood beats here."

Pierce's eyes were the only thing beautiful about his face. They locked onto Jack's. Both of them with the same bright, beautiful eyes. "I'd never leave a wife this farm. No way would I do that, Jack."

Jack smiled. The weight lifted, and he stood up straight.

"But Mimi's only in her early thirties. The two of us want to have children. When that happens, you can be sure they will be getting the farm."

The weight in Jack's stomach should've dropped and shattered. "You're just messing, aren't you? This is one of your weird jokes."

Pierce laughed. He ran his fingertips over his smooth hair. "Do you like the new hair, Jack? Your woman in Boots said it's what all the young fellas use these days." Pierce pulled out his chair and sat down. "Tell you, I'm wrecked before she even gets here. I wonder what I'll be like when she does arrive."

"You're messing, aren't you?" Jack took his cap from his head and wrung it with his hands.

"There are plenty of farmers looking for help around

here if you're wanting a new job. You don't have to stay here. I could always get some young fella, pay him less than I do you and everyone will be happy."

"Pierce?"

"Go on home, Jack," Pierce said. "Mimi is ringing in five minutes."

"I know you're joking with me," Jack said. "I know you'd never do that."

Pierce's eyes were on his phone. The smile on his face was illuminated by the phone's glare.

Jack went into the porch and put his boots back on and closed the door softly behind him. Pierce probably was joking. He was messing when he told Jack to go home. Jack turned around, debating whether to go back. There were plenty of jobs to be done around the farm. He knew he should get started on them or he'd be snookered with them tomorrow. One of his boots crashed through a frozen puddle. He could feel water slipping in the seams, slowly drowning his ruined sock. He pulled his boot free and stepped towards the house. Eyes dancing, he froze once again. Pierce had neglected the farmhouse. Its windows were single-pane and peeling, showing the green paint they had been before their present black, and the roof was so boughed it looked as though it would simply fall through at any moment. While the rest of the farm under Jack's hand was adored. Pierce could feck off for himself. Jack would go home, and he'd stay there until he got an apology and a promise that he'd always be left the farm.

Jack spun around and stomped to his car. His nostrils fumed like a dragon as he drove home.

When Aoife came home later that evening, she was bejewelled with her purchase from Sherry Shines. Her hair was in one of those tight buns that made it look like she had had a facelift. She was smiling until she saw Jack sitting at the kitchen table.

"What are you doing here?" Aoife placed a black bag of coffee granules on the counter.

"Lovely to see you." Jack had changed his clothes when he got home and was wearing his Levi's and the pink jumper that he hated but Aoife liked. It didn't stop her from glaring at the holes in his socks. For Christmas, she had bought him the usual dozen, but he had managed to ruin them. "How was your day, dear?"

"Hectic," Aoife said. "Sarah missed work again, and

guess who had to squeeze in her bookings? Toby saw the state of me and gave me this." Aoife picked up the coffee and smiled at it lovingly. "He's as good, isn't he?"

"I'd love to meet this Toby fella," Jack said. "Give him a new mug for all this coffee." Jack eyed the bag. There was a picture on it of one of those weird skulls that the hipsters got tattoos of. Two people now he wished were skeletons. If only something could happen by wishing it.

"What, you'd actually buy someone something?" Aoife laughed. She fiddled with the coffee machine; Jack had tried making a cup earlier, but the coffee had tasted as bitter as he felt. "And why aren't you milking?" As she said this, she took a litre of slimline milk from the fridge and set it down. "Don't tell me he hired a farmhand."

"Why would you think he hired someone?" Jack asked. All the years now he had worked for Pierce, there'd never been a mention of hiring someone else. Not by Pierce, and most definitely not by Aoife.

"Mary Sullivan's young fella got a call to see if he was interested in working as a farmhand. He's studying agriculture. Mary was telling us all like he was a bloody rocket scientist."

"Who did he get a call from?" Jack asked. The words came out of his mouth fast and hard.

"She didn't say. Why, was it Pierce?"

Jack stood up and walked over to the window. There was a patio outside the window. In summer, when Aoife wasn't working, she'd sit out there. Sometimes he'd join her but more often she'd have her phone for company. Last week, she had mentioned the addition of French doors to make her summer's transitions to the patio easier. Aoife had never brought in the summer cushions from the patio furniture. They had cost a fortune, and now there were black and green spots all over the cream fabric. The wooden patio furniture itself should've been stored in the shed or at least covered and now they were battered from the winter. Jack took accountability for that one, but he'd do the mending on them, too. "He said he'd never leave a wife the farm," Jack said.

"Well, that's good, isn't it?" Aoife opened the pack of her newest bag of coffee and inhaled. "Toby is too good to me. I'll have to leave him a review with his company."

"He's talking about having children with this one, Mimi," Jack said.

Aoife laughed. "Go way out of that. He'd never be

able to get it up. Though I suppose there are pills for that, aren't there, Jack?"

Jack glanced over his shoulder. She had already made herself a cup of coffee and was sipping it with her pinky out. "What's that supposed to mean?"

"Just that anyone could get those pills. Even Pierce. All he'd have to do is go to the doctor." She smiled sweetly. She opened the drawer and pulled out a wad of flyers. "Think I'll order tonight. You want something?"

"He said if they have a child, the farm will go to them and not to me." Jack's eyes were focused on the garden once again. There was a greenhouse out there. A plastic walk-in one that Aoife had purchased while going through her two-week gardening phase. At least she had never lost interest in being a beautician.

"Sure, we might as well get divorced then," Aoife said. She ran her finger down the leaflet. "Too heavy. Too spicy. Just yuck."

"You don't give a shit, do you?" Jack asked. "You really don't."

Aoife laughed. "He's talking out of his arse. You're as bad as him letting it get to you."

"Yesterday, you were all talk about visiting your aunt.

Now, it's just funny."

"We are going to see her." Aoife's finger tapped twice on whatever she had settled on. "Now what are you going to order?"

"What he said, doesn't it worry you?"

"It's the full moon tonight. People are always talking crazy. You're even crazier to believe he's capable of fathering a child."

"The full moon," Jack said, remembering the Jack-in-the-Box. As soon as he got home, he had hidden it away on the top shelf on his side of the wardrobe.

"What food do you want?" She had her phone in her hand and was scrolling through it with her sharp nails scratching against the screen.

"Whatever you're eating," Jack said. He could hear her talking to the restaurant as he left the kitchen. He went into their bedroom, closing the door behind him. There was a canvas of them smiling on their wedding day. Aoife looked gorgeous in her fishtail dress. Her hair smooth as a knife and her eyes wild as the water. When Jack had seen her walking down the aisle, he thought he was dreaming. The dress cost ten grand. It used to be in Aoife's side of the wardrobe before she ordered Jack to send it to the attic. Jack had asked her why she didn't sell it and she didn't speak to him for a week. The suit Jack wore for their big day was bought on Adverts for fifty euros. If Aoife ever found out, she'd burn their marriage certificate.

Jack glanced at the canvas before opening the wardrobe door. Aoife's legs might've looked long but she barely reached five-foot-two. There was no way she'd be able to reach the top shelf without the aid of a stepladder or one of her precious velvet dining chairs. Jack bet her inquisitiveness didn't stretch that far. Jack was six-foot-three. It was no bother for him to reach for the box and pull it towards him. He had only held it yesterday, but still, it was heavier than what he remembered. Shinier too with the gold swirls on the red, just a watt away from shining in the north-facing bedroom. Jack's hand touched the lever. The stallholder was some chancer; Jack knew that but still, what if there was a tiny glob of truth in what he had said? What if the box could somehow stop Pierce's heart? Jack was still in the will. He had seen it himself over Christmas when Pierce had fallen asleep after the drinks of whiskey and the fat dinner. What if there was a way to stop Pierce's life? Wouldn't he be mad not to try it?

Jack went to his car and put the box on the passenger's seat. If he left now, he could still get the milking done. That was if Pierce hadn't started it already. Either way, Jack could finish it. He was speeding away down the road when he remembered Aoife in there, only after ordering food. She'd kill him when he got home, but he'd make it up to her. He'd buy her a bottle of champagne or the like. And he'd buy one for Pierce while he was at it. Anything to keep him on his sweet side.

Fifteen minutes later, Jack pulled up outside the farmhouse with the bottle of champagne in his hand. Pierce was just walking over to the milking parlour when Jack arrived.

"Pierce," Jack called.

"It's the young pup. Coming to beg again, are you?"

"I'm late. I'm sorry. I bought you a bottle of champagne, just to say how happy I am about your news. Sure, I'm only delighted you're getting married."

Pierce had brushed his eyebrows. They were now two tame caterpillars on his face rather than wild, out-of-control ones. Around them, the night was drawing in. "I suppose you're expecting the two of us to sit in there, drinking this together, are you? Just like your father," he added under his breath.

"I'll do the milking; you go in and work your way through it." Jack handed Pierce the bottle of champagne. At first, he thought Pierce would send him packing, but then tight fingers wrapped around the bottle.

"I will so," Pierce said. "It'd be rude if I didn't. I'll send Mimi a picture of the bottle. If I'm feeling generous, I might even leave her a glass."

When Jack had finished the milking, the round moon was watching. It lit up his car, sitting lonely in the yard. Jack turned the lock on the passenger side door. The box was still there. He rubbed his chin, wondering what on earth he had been thinking. Of course, this box wasn't going to do anything. He touched his hand against the lever, but still, he wouldn't turn it.

"What's that you got there?" Pierce was standing in the house's doorway, holding an almost empty glass. "Not another bottle of champagne, is it? I'd only love one. I'd a thirst on me I didn't know I had." He walked over to the car. Jack knew then that his uncle was steaming, seeing the zig-zag of his walk.

"It's nothing," Jack said.

"Don't look like nothing," Pierce said. "Oh, it's a box," he said when he was close enough to see. Pierce snatched it from Jack and carried it into the house. Jack followed him inside without even thinking of taking off his muddy boots. Pierce set the box on the kitchen table and attempted to lift the lid off.

"You can't do that," Jack said.

"Why?" Pierce asked. "What've you got in here, then?" Pierce saw the lever at the side. "Oh, sure, it's one of them Jack-in-the-Boxes. Is it a miniature you inside it? Another little clown of a fella." Jack watched as Pierce turned the lever—the first beat of "Pop Goes the Weasel." Pierce snorted. "I haven't heard this song since I was a young fella." Round and round he turned the lever.

The room was red hot. Jack ran his finger over his lips; they were parched. The bottle of champagne was open on the table. He reached for it and drank it back. Pierce was unaware of Jack's actions. His eyes were glued to the box, and a strange little smile on his lips. Jack took his coat off. It hadn't taken so long to pop at the craft fair. Then, it had appeared within twenty seconds.

"Round and round, I'll sit on me arse. Round and

round, I'll prick you with a needle. Pop goes the…" Up went the Jester. Pierce's singing stopped, and the smile vanished from his face. He grabbed the bottle of champagne from Jack's hands and gulped it. His swallow was loud. "It's an ugly little fecker, isn't it?" Pierce asked. "It must've been modelled on you." He took the box and handed it to Jack. The Jester danced from side to side, its void black eyes ever staring. Jack's hands were sweaty on the box. He pushed the lid down, but his movement was too desperate, and it didn't close properly. The Jester popped straight back up, pushing Jack's hand aside.

"You're a useless little fecker," Pierce said. He watched as Jack wiped his damp hand on his fleece and then pushed the lid down. This time, there was a click.

"You alright?" Jack asked.

"You talking to me or your little friend in the box?" Pierce asked. His face was flushed red, but the parts of his skin that didn't have the look of a tomato were garishly white. "Cause I'm in grand form with this champagne you got me. It's not even the cheap stuff."

Jack scratched his cheek. His whole body was itchy. Something that always happened whenever he was anxious. When he started dating Aoife, she taught him better ways to manage his anxiety rather than making her look like a complete fool when she brought him out in public. "I better go. I'll see you in the morning."

"Unless I'm dead," Pierce laughed.

"Why would you say that?" Jack snapped. "Course you won't be dead."

"You'd only love that, though, wouldn't you?" Pierce said. "Maybe I should be worried that you're after putting poison into my champagne. I watch them true crime videos on YouTube. I know how it works." Pierce winked. He took the champagne and drank. "I'm only messing with you, Jacky Boy. I know you'd be too much of a wuss to do any such thing."

Jack nodded. "I'll see you in the morning. Have a good one."

"Have a good one, he says. Oh, I will have a good one. It'll be even better when Mimi gets here." Pierce took up his phone and scrolled with his stubby finger.

There was a tint of red to the moon. Jack hadn't stepped into a church since his confirmation, but still, he blessed himself. He put the Jack-in-the-Box into the boot and drove home.

Aoife was sitting on the L-shaped couch, which was far too big for the small living room. The walls in here were white like the rest of the cottage. There was an empty wine glass on the coffee table and a candle that was meant to smell like clean linen. Jack didn't mind the smell, but it always scratched at his sinuses.

"There you are," Aoife said when Jack entered the room. She had the lights off, and only the TV and that sinus-hating candle gave light to the room. She was in her dressing gown now, with her hair in one of those messy knots on top of her head. "I thought you were after running away to be with your cows."

"Oh, I did," Jack said. "I was. I finished doing the milking. Sorry, I ran off the way I did. You know me when I get into a panic. I'd hate for Pierce to get some young fella doing my job. There was no one there anyway. No one but Pierce."

"And the cows," Aoife said. Her eyes stayed glued to the screen. Only when Jack told her he had bought champagne did she unglue them and look at the bottle that he had placed on the table.

On the TV screen was one of those reality shows with

people on a beach. Jack could never understand why she watched it. Anytime he tried to join her, he'd be snoring within minutes.

"Are you hungry?" Aoife asked.

"I am a bit," Jack said.

"Your Chinese is in the fridge. Go and heat it and it'll still be grand."

"I will so," Jack said.

"Thanks for this," Aoife said, placing the bottle on the table.

"You're welcome," Jack said. He was hoping she'd open it and offer him a glass, but she did no such thing. When the show was over, Aoife did a bit of scrolling on her phone before heading to bed. Jack followed her shortly after, his belly uncomfortably full of Chinese food. Aoife turned to her side and slept peacefully on the expensive bed linen. Jack's mind swirled. He thought of the Jack-in-the-Box alone in the boot of the car and Pierce all alone for years in that big farmhouse. Mostly Jack thought how stupid he had been, bringing the toy with him to Pierce. Even if it did as Jackser promised, Jack wouldn't want Pierce to die, would he? A little whispery voice inside his head that sounded just like Jackser said, *yes, oh yes, yes.*

***

Jack woke up the next morning before the alarms went off on his phone. His body was so accustomed to getting up at the same time every day that an alarm was no longer needed; still, he set it. Missing the milking was something he had nightmares about. He crept out of bed. Aoife would be up now, shortly after him. She didn't start work until 9 but she was a mad woman for her early morning HITT classes. Jack knew she was awake even then, but she liked to pretend she wasn't. Let her be. He needed his peace as much as she needed hers.

It was the peace that Jack loved most about these early mornings. It was a great feeling to be awake when so many people were still sleeping. Jack had all the peace he could want until he arrived at the farm and Pierce would be gawking out of the kitchen window, waiting for him to arrive. Some days he mightn't be staring but you'd know he was there with some shadow of him visible in the dim light. Only that day there was no sign of him.

Jack parked the car and got out. He walked slowly across the yard. The moon was still there in the sky. He had seen it on the drive over, but it was no longer shining on this side of the house. He was in near darkness with only the slightest stirring in the night sky. Jack pressed down on the latch, but the door didn't open. Not once, not even when Pierce had taken to his bed during the first round of COVID-19, had this happened.

Jack knocked at the door. "Pierce?" he called.

No answer.

"Pierce?" he said, louder this time.

Still, there was no answer.

Jack himself didn't have a key. Pierce had said there was no need, but he'd leave a copy under the seat of the old tractor at the back of the house. Jack went to the side of the house. Here, he could see the moon and her light shining onto the rusted, decaying tractor. *Crunch* went the stones as Jack walked over them. *Splash* went the puddles he stepped into. He arrived at the tractor and pried the rusted door open. When Jack was a child, he used to play in the tractor. That had all stopped when a rusted nail went through his Power Ranger wellies and into his foot. After that, the tractor had been off-limits. Jack reached underneath the seat and patted the cold ground. Something with bristly fur touched against his finger and then ran out of the door.

"Jesus Christ," Jack said. His mind went to Jackser. *That's not Jesus Christ; that's a rat.* "Rat a tat tat, break your mother's back," Jack whispered. Cold fingers ran down his spine, and he shivered. Jack glanced behind him at the house. Still not a peep of light. "If you're not dead, I'll kill you." There was a branch that had fallen from the tree overhead, lying on the frosted grass. Jack picked it up and hit it against the tractor's floor. When no nibbling rats ran out, he closed his eyes and reached for the key. He felt the cold metal and pulled it out with sweaty fingers. Jack slammed the tractor door and made his way to the house.

Still, no light as he worked the key in the lock. A little *click* and it opened. It was even darker inside the porch than it was outside. Jack flipped the switch. The light came on for a few seconds before dying with a sizzle a few beats later.

"Pierce?" Jack called as he walked into the kitchen. No answer. But the light worked in here, drowning out the clean kitchen in a dim glow. It was perfect for when the kitchen was filthy, but now with it cleaner, it just made everything look half-alive. Everything but Pierce, who lay on his back on the floor, staring at the ceiling. His eyes were open. Jack was no fool; he knew his uncle was dead. Still, he called his name. "Pierce, Pierce, Pierce." Jack dropped to his knees and checked for a pulse. Nothing. Stone cold. The look on his face was frozen. Eyes wide, mouth open. Pierce had died alone and terrified. Jack's back cracked when he stood up. He saw the empty bottle of champagne on the table and an ashtray littered with butts. Pierce's phone was between them. Jack picked it up, intending to call an ambulance. He didn't mean to press on the message from Mimi. A WhatsApp thread appeared on the screen. The last message had come from Mimi at 10. p.m.

Mimi: **Please you stop message me. I love another man**.

Jack scrolled through the messages. Last week she had professed her love for Pierce and asked for 20,000 euros to organise flights to Ireland and get herself ready for the trip. Pierce had sent the money. She told him she'd arrive yesterday. Then yesterday, it had changed to next week.

Pierce: **Can we video chat, Mimi, darling?**

Mimi: **I'm no able to talk. I change my mind. I'm not coming to Ireland.**

There was a string of messages from Pierce, all of

them begging for Mimi to talk with him. Silence from Mimi, and then the dead silence from Pierce.

"Oh, Jesus," Jack said. "Jesus, Jesus, Jesus." Jackser's voice in his head. *Not Jesus but your dead uncle. Ring an ambulance, Jacky Boy, and see if they can absolve you of your sins.*

Jack rang the ambulance. They arrived twenty minutes later. A sad shake of the head from a young fella with dark hair and a square jaw. "He's gone," the young fella whispered.

What Jack wanted to say was: "He's not gone. Sure, I can see him right there," but he just bowed his head and kept quiet. Jack didn't say much of anything when Pierce was loaded onto the stretcher and brought into the ambulance. When the other paramedic, a woman with short, dark hair, glanced at Jack's car, Jack swore she knew what was inside the boot. When the ambulance drove away with the lights as dead as Pierce, he knew it was just paranoia getting to him.

Alone now, he walked to the boot and opened it. The Jack-in-the-Box was just where he had left it. Innocent as Christmas. Only, when Jack placed his hand on top of the box, he swore he could feel the pulse that was absent from Pierce. Jack slammed the boot down. This was madness. It was just a coincidence. A nasty bloody coincidence.

He rang Aoife. When she didn't answer, he went into the parlour and got on with the milking. They were happy to see him, the cows; his cows now.

When Aoife lived in Dublin, before she had met Jack, she did a part-time acting course at the Gaiety School of Acting. All Jack could think when he told her about Pierce's passing was that those acting lessons must've paid off because you'd think she had been mad about Pierce. When she called to the farm an hour later, she cried as she hugged Jack, but Jack could see the new way she looked at the farmhouse, as if she were doing a checklist of everything she needed to do.

"Will I make you a cup of tea?" Aoife asked.

"I'd murder a cup of tea," Jack said. His heart beat something wicked. "Not murder; I mean I'd kill for one." Jack rubbed the edge of his index finger against his lips. "I'd love one is all I mean to say."

Together they walked into the kitchen. It was cold in there without the stove burning. Aoife's white runners had been covered with mud on the walk from the car to the door. She left them side-by-side with Jack's boots on the porch.

"You'll have to light that." Aoife nodded at the stove. "You'll have visitors coming here until you're up to your eyes with them." Jack lit the stove as Aoife made them tea. Jack had already done a clean-up of the kitchen so that the only thing that remained of Pierce from the night before was the slight dent in the seat cushion. This dent disappeared as soon as Jack sat down in what had always been his uncle's place.

"Are you okay?" Aoife asked in a soothing voice. Jack wondered if this was the voice that she used on clients after she had stripped them of their body hair. She placed the cup of tea on the table and touched the top of Jack's arm.

"It was a bit of a shock, not going to lie." Jack drank his tea.

"It was," Aoife said. "Of course, it was." She grimaced when she tasted her tea—missing her usual machine coffee.

They hadn't yet finished their cups when Mary O'Shea, the nearest neighbour, called around with a stew in a red casserole dish. She was the first of many who called around that day, most of them bearing a food offering. Jack accepted their condolences. Aoife did the talking while simultaneously organising the funeral. All Jack had to do was ring one of the local pubs to see if they could serve soup and sandwiches after the funeral. He was delighted when they said yes and dismayed when he learnt the cost. But it didn't matter now, did it? The farm was his, this house was his, he could afford to pay.

By the time Jack had finished the second milking, an assortment of people had called to the farmhouse. Only three of them Jack recognised, never mind knew their names. When Jack had done everything he needed to do on the farm, he and Aoife went back to their house. He hadn't wanted to leave the farm on its own, but Aoife convinced him to return, at least just for that night.

Later, in the deep night, Jack snuck out of the house and went to his car. The boot was stiff to open. It reminded Jack of the tractor's door. The rat was the horror in there. Jack opened the boot and there was the Jack-in-the-Box. Was that the horror here?

Jack didn't know he was humming the tune of "Pop

Goes the Weasel" until he heard the faraway dog barking. He wasn't sure whose dog it even was. It might have been Mary O'Shea's, who bought two big fellas after her had husband passed. He stopped humming, disgusted with himself, when Pierce was turning to stone in Hennessy's funeral home. That was where he'd remain until his funeral. There'd be no wake in the house for Pierce. Oh no, there wouldn't.

Jack picked up the box. He dropped it when he thought he felt the pulse again. The moon was above him, a day past its full point, but you'd still think it was as full as ever. Jack picked up the box again. His fingers touched the lever. He wondered, if he were to turn it now, would he go the way Pierce had? Jack slammed the boot. This was madness. The box hadn't done anything. He hadn't done anything. He went into the house, tiptoed into the bedroom, and returned the small Jack to the tallest shelf.

Only, when sleep's hand was about to claim him, he thought he heard the pulsing coming from inside the wardrobe and his eyes bolted open. They stayed this way for most of the night, until at some point he fell asleep and woke to Aoife shaking him.

"Your first day being the owner and you're sleeping

in?" Aoife said. Her tone was jovial, but the words pierced Jack's heart.

Jack jumped from the bed and drove so fast to the farm that he skidded on the road. All was well on the farm, and he got straight to the milking. Aoife might've been joking but Jack's mind was made up. There'd be no more sleeping in the cottage for him. He was the owner now and a farmer belonged on their farm.

Aoife called around after the morning milking. Ready for life on the farm, she had traded her white runners for hot pink wellies.

"You're not working today?" Jack asked. He saw her looking at the ground.

"We're going to have to do something about the state of this. It's like living in a bloody pig stye. And no, I'm not working. Sure, I'm running around like a mad woman trying to get everything sorted. Speaking of which, we're going to need a suit for Pierce."

"For Pierce?" Jack said. "What's he going to need a suit for?"

"His funeral?" Aoife said.

Jack smacked his palm against his forehead. "God,

yeah, I'm some—I'm just tired, I guess. I didn't get all that much sleep last night. Hopefully, I'll sleep better tonight."

"So, you are sleeping here then?" Aoife asked.

"I will," Jack said. "I'll have to from now on. It would be madness leaving it on its own."

"I suppose you're right," Aoife said. "Sooner the better, we get the cottage on the market and then we can get started on this place. It'll be some home by the time I'm finished with it. Now, we better get looking for this suit of his."

It had been years since Jack had gone upstairs in the house. There was never any need. The furthest he had ventured was the downstairs toilet. Even then, he had felt like he was intruding on Pierce's space. Aoife had no qualms about the invasion. She walked into the kitchen and opened the ancient white door that led to the hallway. The tiles on the floor were blue and yellow and looked like a leftover of the Victorian age. Jack had always liked them, but he knew that Aoife would want to rip them up during the renovation. The door on the other side of the hallway led to a sitting room that hadn't been used in decades. To the right was the bathroom with a shower installed in the 80s for Jack's ailing granny, who used to sleep in one of the other rooms downstairs. Aoife led the way; her footsteps were light on the deep blue carpet that was in dire need of a vacuum but otherwise looked in decent shape.

Upstairs now. The lower half of the walls were wood-panelled, while the top half was covered with yellow wallpaper. On the walls were various family pictures. Jack spotted a picture of him on his first communion, standing between his parents. Between pictures and wallpaper were five doors. The one at the end of the hallway led to a bathroom, while the other four led to bedrooms. Jack hadn't a clue which one Pierce slept in. It didn't take long to find out. Two of the rooms were empty save for brass iron single beds without any linen. One room had a double bed without a mattress. The last room had a single bed with a thin pillow and three scratchy blue blankets. Next to the bed was a bedside table with a couple of Farmers Weekly magazines. There was a 70s-style wardrobe and a matching chest of drawers. Aoife confidently marched across the brown carpet with yellow flowers and inspected the contents of the wardrobe.

"Where do you think he was going to put Mimi?" Jack

asked. He had already told Aoife about the messages he'd seen on Pierce's phone.

"Sure, she was never coming here," Aoife said. As she pushed her way through clothes, the hangers scratched against the pole.

"But when he thought that she was. Sure, he was preparing for her visit."

"Maybe he was planning on squeezing her in that bed with him," Aoife laughed. "Honestly, the things you think about."

The brown curtains were open, revealing a beautiful day outside. Jack gazed out on his land, thinking of all the things he would do with it. In the distance, he could see Mary O'Shea's cottage and her few acres. Maybe he could even buy her land in time. It wasn't like she was doing anything with it.

"Here we are." Aoife retrieved a grey suit from the wardrobe. "Think this is the one he wore to our wedding. It will be perfect." She shut the wardrobe door.

"It will be," Jack said. He could remember Pierce in that suit at their wedding. He had drunk his way through the free wine and spent much of the night dancing with one of the bridesmaids. They had all looked the same to

Jack in their satiny dresses and fancy hairstyles.

"Well, I better bring it to the funeral home," Aoife said. She walked out of the room and Jack followed. He left the door for Pierce's bedroom open, and the light pouring from the room illuminated the damp spots on the wallpaper. The stairs creaked when they walked down them. Jack could remember that creak when he was a little boy, and his granny saying it was just the house stretching its bones.

Back in the kitchen, Jack looked at the stove. There'd be little point in lighting it today. All those paying their respects would meet later at the funeral home.

"I'll see you this evening then," Aoife said.

"You won't stay for some food?" Jack asked.

"I'd love to, but I need to bring this suit in, or else Pierce will be displayed in the nip. I can't ask you to bring it in when I know you're up to your ears now around here." She smiled. "But I'll see you later."

When Aoife left, Jack cleaned out the bedroom with the double bed frame. When the room was relatively clean, he dragged two single mattresses from the other bedrooms and put them on the empty frame. He found bedlinen, a bit musty smelling but not in the worst shape, and made up the bed.

Before it was time to do the second milking, he drove to the cottage. The sun was glaring in the sky, and he had to use his sunglasses to avoid being completely blinded by it. Aoife's car wasn't there. Jack didn't know he had been looking forward to seeing her until he felt the disappointment at her absence. Nevertheless, he went inside. She must've been burning a new scent of those expensive candles because there was a strange smell in the air that he didn't recognise. She was always buying those candles. She used to have them lit in different rooms simultaneously before Jack begged her to keep it limited to the one room.

Jack went into the bedroom. Aoife had left his black suit on the bed and his good shoes on the blanket box at the end of the bed. He had last worn them in the summer, when one of Aoife's colleagues was getting married. It was one of the most boring weddings that Jack had ever been to until there was a punch-up with a groomsman and one of the serving staff.

Jack smiled at the memory as he opened the wardrobe door. The smile was wiped clean when he saw the glint of red and gold on the top shelf. He reached for the box. He could feel the smooth, cold surface and what felt like the trace of a pulse underneath. Jack pushed the box away. It slid until it came to a soft landing—probably hitting against a pile of long-forgotten t-shirts that had been stored away for the summer at some point. This was madness. That bloody chancer had put stupid thoughts into his head. It was more likely the man was one of those psychics than the box could hurt anyone. Jack laughed. Alone in the house, he thought he sounded like a madman.

He took the little suitcase from the bottom of the wardrobe, zipped it open, and packed it with supplies for the night. When he was finished packing, he carried everything out to the car. As he pulled the door closed, he noticed the earth had broken in the pink pots outside the front door and the daffodils were finally rising. At long last, spring had come.

Jack started the second milking earlier than he usually would. When it was finished, he jumped into the old electric shower downstairs. It was yellowing, and the knob for temperature control was stiff to turn but it worked. Only, the shower was so loud that Jack's thoughts were full of people being fried to death as they showered. He'd have to get the wiring checked in the house. That would be one of the first things he'd do once the funeral was over. He had forgotten to bring a towel with him and had to use one of Pierce's. There were holes in it and its eighties-style design was now faded into a blur, but it did the job. When he was dry, he got into his suit and inspected himself in the mirror. He looked well; this was the Jack that Aoife admired. She'd have him wearing a suit every day if she could.

Aoife was inside the funeral home when he got there. Soon the mourners would file in. He had already seen a few of them donning black and chattering outside. Aoife was sitting on a stiff-looking white chair with her legs crossed. She smiled when she saw him. She wore a tight black dress that he'd never seen her wear before. Aoife rarely wore black. Even at work, she was only in bright colours. But the black suited her. She was bright enough as it was; having all that colour on her only made it too difficult to look at her.

"Just the slightest bit of mud on your shoes," Aoife said, smiling. "How did you manage that? I was worried you'd have your suit ruined."

"It wasn't easy," Jack said. It wasn't; he had had to tiptoe to the car, making him feel more of a prat than he already did.

"Are you ready to see him?" Aoife stood up. She was wearing a pair of high-heeled shoes that looked more like weapons than footwear. Still, she was no skyscraper and only came to Jack's shoulder.

"See who?" Jack asked, looking around the room. It was very Aoife, with the white walls and burning candles. When he saw the coffin at the top of the room, he knew who she was talking about.

"The King of the Magpies, always on his own," Aoife said. She walked to the coffin.

Jack wondered if her stilettos would leave wounds on the wooden floor. He would've looked but his eyes were glued to the coffin. He expected that Pierce's mouth and eyes would still be open, frozen in the terror that he had died in. He hadn't expected that they would be closed and that Pierce's usually stern and cranky face would look at peace. Only in death, Pierce could relax, and there was even a slight tilt of his lips to make it look as though he was smiling. Not Pierce's usual contemptuous smile but one that wished joy for the beholder. Although Jack knew it was the work of the embalmer, it was that smile that eased away any of his remaining anxieties over Pierce's death. Jack touched his hand against Pierce's marble one. Aoife placed her hand over Jack's, and it was there they stood as the first of the mourners entered the room.

The evening went smoothly. Far more people than either Aoife or Jack had expected turned up and shook their hands. Many commented on how well Pierce looked. One woman with a pearl-coloured perm commented that death suited him. Jack had to agree. It was a shame that Pierce hadn't died earlier.

When the last of the mourners had gone home, Jack and Aoife went back to the farmhouse and ate lasagna and apple tart. At eight p.m., Aoife announced it was time for her to return home. When Jack asked if she would stay, she refused but said she might the following night. He knew she wouldn't by the way she said *might*. Aoife either wanted to do something or she didn't—any form of hesitation usually pointed to her indifference.

Jack walked Aoife to her car. "I'll miss you tonight," he said.

Aoife smiled at him as she got into the car. "You're as good."

Jack stood there with his hands in his pockets, watching her drive away. Then it was just him and the waning moon. It was losing that round shape now; you'd know it was on the way to disappearing. He'd have to get some spotlights out here—those motion detector ones. He used to get on to Pierce to install them, but after years of saying it to him, Jack had given up. When tomorrow was over, there'd be a lot to do. Jackser's voice whispered in his head. *Get rid of the body and reap the rewards*. Jack silenced the voice with loud footsteps as he walked into the house.

He glanced around the kitchen. It was like being in a dream, the most surreal of dreams. It had all happened so fast. Waiting and waiting for years, and now here it was. All things in life seemed to be like that—all the things you really wanted anyway. Now this house, twice as big as the cottage and with a million more memories, was his. He made himself a cup of tea and sat at the table. He and Aoife's dishes were still there. He'd every intention of cleaning them before going to sleep but when the yawning started, he left them where they were and went to bed.

As he lay on the sagging mattress, feeling the spring dig into his back, he didn't think there'd be much of a chance that he would sleep. He was used to the warmth of the cottage. Without the stove heating the radiators in the house, it was cold. Not only was it cold, but it creaked and ached in a way that the cottage didn't. Regardless of the cold and the creaking, Jack did fall asleep, and it was peaceful and dreamless.

***

Jack met Aoife at the funeral home the next day. Aoife's parents were away in Spain so they wouldn't be there, but her sister Veronica, with big hair and pink lips, was. The constant laughing must have been hereditary because Veronica was giggling away at something. Aoife for once was serious-looking but she smiled when she saw Jack. Her hair was in one of those vintage-style waves and she had a black beret that was adorned with jewels. Jack wondered if they were real. Knowing Aoife, it wouldn't surprise him.

"How did you sleep then?" Aoife asked him. There were bits of white on his suit coat; she picked them off and flicked them on the ground. "Did you see any ghosts?"

"Is that why you wouldn't stay?" Jack asked.

"No ghosts, then?" Aoife asked.

"None," Jack said.

Together, they walked into the funeral parlour. They took one more look at Pierce and waited outside for the coffin to be transported to the hearse. Twenty other people joined them outside the parlour, including a distant cousin Jack thought had died a decade ago. The cousin, Miriam, was pale enough to be a ghost, and Jack even entertained the notion until he saw her talking to a very loud man who was the epitome of life.

When the coffin was safe inside the hearse, Jack and Aoife got into the shiny black car that the funeral parlour had supplied. There, sitting in the backseat together, Aoife presented a wad of papers. "I've highlighted the prayers that you're going to say. Will you be alright saying them?"

"I will," Jack said.

And he was. Although his hand shook, he spoke loudly and clearly. Later, after Pierce was lowered into the ground, a lady with a purple rinse and a huge grey jacket that made her slim frame look large, congratulated Jack on his recitation. "He would've been proud of you," the lady said. She gripped Jack's hand tight enough that Jack could feel her rings digging into him. "Course he was proud of you. He was mad about you, he was. He'd always be talking about you." When Jack smelled the faint aroma of whiskey coming from her, he knew he was talking with Lucy Power. Pierce would mention her from time to time or, more specifically. the whiskey always steaming from her. "It was a sad, lonely life but at least he had you." Lucy's fierce green eyes stared into Jack's. "Never forget how much he loved you." A final squeeze of the hand and Lucy cleared away. When she did, Jack saw Aoife talking to a tall, muscular-looking man with his blonde hair tied in what Aoife called a protective bun. Not just talking to him—oh, no. Aoife was gazing up at him in the way that she used to do with Jack when they first started dating. When the two of them hugged, Jack bolted over.

Even though it was Jack's uncle's funeral, Aoife seemed surprised to see Jack. "Jack," she said, her eyes wide. "You gave me a fright."

"I think it's hard not to be frightened in a graveyard," the man said.

"This is Toby," Aoife said. She had one arm on Toby and her body tilted towards Jack.

"I finally get to meet the famous Toby," Jack said. "I've heard lots about you." When Toby stuck out his hand, Jack shook it and squeezed.

"Sorry to hear about your uncle," Toby said. His eyes were bright blue and watery. They looked as though they had been transported from a much older person into a young man's body. And he was young. Jack had been expecting Toby to be somewhere in his forties, not this young fella who looked no more than twenty-five.

"Thanks," Jack said. Before he could exchange any more words with Toby, he was pulled away by a short man in a bowler hat who wouldn't let go of Jack's hand as he offered his condolences. When the man finally let go of Jack's hand, Aoife was standing on her own, watching Jack. Jack went over to her. "Awful good of your delivery driver to come to the funeral of someone he doesn't know."

"He came for me," Aoife said. "Pierce was my uncle-in-law."

"The two of ye couldn't stand each other," Jack said.

"Who couldn't stand each other?" Veronica strolled

over to them. She had added more lipstick, but it didn't hide the chapped lips underneath. "Is someone starting a fight?" She widened her eyes. She had clumped on the mascara, and her lashes reminded Jack of spider legs.

"We better get to Doyle's," Aoife said. "Most of them are already over there." She linked Veronica and the two of them strolled ahead of Jack. Jack thought it was just as well that Veronica lived in Cork; the thought of seeing her more than twice a year was as appealing as dancing with the dead.

At the pub, Veronica sat with them. In between mouthfuls of soup and sandwiches, Veronica spoke of nothing but her children. When she had cleared her food, she looked from Aoife to Jack. "So now that the two of ye will have that big farmhouse, you'll have to start filling it with children, won't ye?"

Jack swallowed his egg and cress. "We might just get some dogs. Sure, they're as good as children, aren't they? And not nearly half as annoying."

Aoife glared at him from across the table. He wasn't sure what she was annoyed about when she wasn't keen on reproducing either. Veronica laughed but there was little joy in it. When she went to the bar a few minutes later, Aoife sat forward with her blouse hitting off the side of a sandwich, leaving a blob of yellow on the white. "Whatever poison you're after swallowing, will you spit it out?"

"Coming from the one who flirts with a young fella after her husband's uncle has been buried," Jack said.

"I wasn't flirting with anyone," Aoife said in a stage whisper. "I was only hugging my friend. If you spent more time away from your cows, you'd know friends hug each other."

Jack gritted his teeth but didn't say anything further. When Veronica came back, she had a story to tell after hearing it from someone at the bar. Jack excused himself and ordered a pint of Guinness. He made small talk with a blonde-haired woman and sipped his pint. When the white head was at the bottom of the glass, all the soup and sandwiches had been consumed and people were leaving the pub.

Veronica brought Aoife and Jack

to their cars, which were still outside of the funeral home. Jack thanked Veronica for coming. Aoife hugged her sister. And they both went into their separate cars and drove away.

When Jack arrived at the cottage, Aoife's Sportage was in the driveway but there was no sign of her in the driver's seat. Jack went into the house and found her in the kitchen, making a cup of coffee.

"Hey," he said. "Were you racing me back?"

"It wouldn't be hard to race you with that piece of shit you're driving," Aoife said. She added sweetener and Slimline milk to her coffee. "But it would be hard to race you when I didn't even know you were coming here."

"Don't I live here?" Jack asked.

"You live at the farm now, just like you've always wanted." Aoife turned around and faced him, holding her cup of coffee between them.

"I'm sorry for getting jealous, if that's what you're upset about," Jack said.

Aoife sighed. She went to say something but then stopped. "Alright."

"Just alright?" Jack asked. "Not going to give me a big lecture?"

"It's been a long few days. I'm tired. You're tired. I'm in no mood to fight. I hardly think you are either."

"I'm not," Jack said.

"Grand." Aoife sipped her coffee. "We'll leave it at

that so." She sat at the kitchen table and stared out the window. "I'll get the auctioneers in here next week and get the place valued."

"Yeah?" Jack asked. "That would be great to get a move on things. The sooner this place is sold, the sooner you can start working on the house." Jack checked the time on his watch. Just after two now; there was still a bit of time before the second milking. "I suppose I better start bringing more of my things over there. No point in leaving them here."

Aoife nodded. "I suppose there isn't."

Jack's holdall was still at the farmhouse, so he took a bin bag from under the sink and brought it with him into the bedroom. There was a clean linen candle beside the bed, with the wax inside midway down the glass. Jack's sinuses tingled. He opened the window, letting in a draft of clean, cool air, and immediately felt better. After emptying his socks and jocks from the drawers, he opened the wardrobe. There was no point in leaving the Jack-in-the-Box there. He couldn't use one of Aoife's good velvet chairs now or she'd kill him, so Jack took the flimsy stool in front of the dressing table and stood on that as he dragged the box towards himself. Jack pressed his hand flat on top of the box. There was nothing, not a beat. Course, the whole business had been nonsense. Jack threw the box in on top of what he had already gathered and then filled the rest of the bag with clothes. When he went back into the kitchen, Aoife was smiling her head off.

"There must've been a lot more than caffeine in that coffee to have you smiling so much," Jack said.

"I've been looking up property prices around here. Some of them are selling for twice as much as what we paid for this place."

"Let's hope we're as lucky," Jack said.

Aoife set her phone down on the table. "How long do you reckon until it's all in your name?"

"I don't know," Jack said. It was true. He hadn't a clue. "Hopefully it won't take too long."

Jack made himself a cup of tea. Whatever tension remained from their earlier fight vanished as they browsed through houses in the local area. When Jack had finished his tea, he put the empty mug into the dishwasher. "I don't suppose you're going to stay at the farm tonight, are you?"

"I won't tonight, but maybe I will tomorrow."

"Hopefully." Jack took up his black sack and walked to the car. Aoife waved to him at the door.

Later that evening, when the milking was complete, Jack unpacked the bag and left the clothes in the old wardrobe in his room. The box didn't go in his wardrobe this time. Although Jack knew he had only been fearful before, he still didn't want that thing anywhere near him. What he did was bring it into the sitting room. The door squeaked as he opened it. Jack flipped the switch, and a dim light filled the room. In the centre of the room were two sofas facing each other. In between them was a coffee table. On top of the table was an ashtray with a cigarette butt smashed into the glass. At the back of the room, in front of the sofas, was the fireplace. There was a gold fire screen in front of the fireplace and a matching gold coal bucket. On one side of the fireplace was a piano, and on the other was a dresser. There were stacks of books and bottles of wine on the dresser; all of them were gathering dust. On the lower part of the dresser were two doors. Jack opened them. There was an array of dust-covered delph and an old box that had once been Jack's granny's sewing box. Jack took out the sewing box, pushed the

Jack-in-the-Box to the back and put the sewing box in front. He closed the doors and stood up. Now, it was all forgotten about.

***

Six weeks after Pierce's funeral, Jack got the phone call from his solicitor asking him to sign the final papers. Jack smiled all the way there. He had done a lot of smiling since Pierce had died. Living in the house made life easier. Being able to go to work and not have snide comments as a constant soundtrack made it peaceful. As for the farm itself, it was thriving. Even the cows seemed much happier without Pierce. Aoife was in great form too, and she was as full of plans as ever. She had arranged for the estate agents to visit their cottage, and they had estimated the property's value as thrice as what they had paid for it. Perhaps the only downside in the last six weeks was Aoife's reluctance to spend nights at the farmhouse. But she had stayed over for a couple of nights and promised that as soon as their house was on the market, she'd start work on the farmhouse and would have no problem staying then.

Leaving the solicitor's after signing the papers, Jack was smiling even wider now. The farmhouse and the farm were now officially his. Years dreaming of this moment, and it was finally here. There was a lightness to his step as he walked to the beautician's, where Aoife worked. He opened the door and was hit with the same array of scents that always made his eyes water and his nose run.

Aoife was standing behind the counter in her pink and black tunic. She had chopped her hair a month ago and it was now in a graduated bob that was needle-sharp at the front. "Jack?" she asked.

They were the same keys that he had been using for the last six weeks, but Jack shook them in the air. "Guess who's the official owner of the farm now?"

"Are you serious?" Aoife asked, coming out from behind the counter.

"I am," Jack said.

The owner of the beautician's, Olivia, a tall, blonde woman with green eyes, walked over to them. "Well, I suppose congratulations are in order then to the pair of ye. Go on off out of here, Aoife, and have a glass of champagne on me."

"Are you sure?" Aoife asked.

"You finished your bookings for the day. Course I'm sure," Olivia said.

Aoife didn't need to be told twice. She took her white coat from the hook, put it on, and left the beautician's. They went for a celebratory meal, bought a bottle of champagne, and went to the farm.

The kitchen was warm from the fire the previous night but still Jack lit the stove. Aoife watched him, running her hands up and down her arms. That was one of the excuses for not wanting to stay at the house, citing how cold it was.

"You won't be able to give out about the cold here tonight with this roaring," Jack said. Aoife had promised that she'd spend the night and would help Jack drink every last drop of champagne.

Aoife didn't say anything. Instead, she picked up the champagne from the table. "You opening this, or will I?"

"I will." Jack took the bottle. He turned it around in his hands and inspected the label. It was a different brand than the one Pierce had drunk on his final few hours on earth. Just as well, Jack didn't think he'd be able to stomach drinking the same type. He hadn't even paid much attention to the champagne in the off-license, just paid for the one that Aoife had picked out. "The house will have to go on the market now," Jack said. "We'll get onto the estate agent first thing Monday morning."

"You going to stand there talking about the estate agents or open that thing?" Aoife asked. She moved closer to the stove, and the fire burning inside the glass lit up her face.

"Your patience was one of the first things I loved about you." Jack opened the bottle and filled Aoife's glass first and then his own. "So will I ring, or will you?"

"Ring who?" Aoife asked. There was a little beep from her phone, and she took it out from her pink handbag.

"The estate agents," Jack said.

Aoife's face paled. She bit the nail on her thumb. "I'm going to have to go," she said.

"Go where?" Jack asked. "Don't tell me there's some old biddy looking for a Brazilian, is there?"

"It's Veronica. She's having a bit of an issue with Declan and wants to talk about it with me. She's after leaving Cork and wants me to go and meet her."

"Couldn't she not ring you like a normal person?" Jack asked. The bubbles in his mouth didn't taste so good anymore.

"She never does this. Whatever's going on must be a big deal for her to want to meet." Aoife picked up her handbag from the table.

"Well, it's still early. When the two of ye are finished talking, come back here and we can still drink the champagne."

"By the time I drive halfway to her, chat, and then drive back, it'll be far too late for me to drink any champagne. And it wouldn't surprise me if she's going to want to come back and stay."

"Well, why doesn't she just drive straight to you now instead of making you drive halfway?"

"Honestly, Jack. Veronica never does this. For all I know, she mightn't even want to stay. I'm just saying that might happen. You work away on the champagne, and we'll celebrate together another night."

"I will so," Jack said.

"No need to look so moody. If it was the other way around, I'd understand."

Jack knew she wouldn't. "Well, I'll see you later or tomorrow, if the worst comes to it." He drank what was left in his glass and when he heard Aoife's car drive away, he drank her mostly full glass. After the second milking, Jack finished the bottle. He mightn't be much of a drinker, but he could hold his alcohol when he did drink.

After finishing the bottle of champagne, Jack was buzzed but by no means drunk. He would've loved another bottle but couldn't drive. He had the phone to his ear, ready to ring in a delivery order for the carryout, when he remembered the bottles of wine that he had seen on the dresser in the sitting room. Jack entered the space. He still hadn't gotten around to oiling the door and it squeaked on its hinges. Inside the room it was cold. Jack checked the radiators. They were warm on the bottom and cold on the top. A simple bleeding is all they would need. He should've checked them all as soon as he moved in, but he had spent such little time in this room that it was like it didn't even exist. Nevertheless, he went to the dresser and took a bottle. He wasn't the biggest wine fan, but when he did indulge, he'd always go for red. There was no cork on the bottle but there was a screw top; he unscrewed it and drank.

Jack surveyed the sitting room. He wondered if Pierce ever sat in it. Probably not. It, unlike the kitchen, felt too lonely. It was a room for entertaining, for families, not for a man on his own. It made the loneliness too consuming. In the kitchen, with the heat of the stove and the simple goings-on of the day, you could forget the emptiness. Jack laughed at himself. He was being morose. He wasn't on his own. He had Aoife. Pierce had been the lonely one. Lived on his own, died on his own, clutching onto a bottle. A heart attack; tick tock and the clock stopped.

It had nothing to do with the Jack-in-the-Box. Jack told himself this anytime the dark voice inside his head started whispering. Jack tried to pretend that it didn't even exist. Yet standing there, such a feat was impossible. He left his wine on top of the dresser, pulled the sewing box out, and removed the Jack-in-the-Box. His hand went to the lever. The moon was only a sliver in the sky, no need to be afraid. Jack turned the lever. The first note of "Pop Goes the Weasel" danced around the room. Jack exhaled as if he were blowing out smoke. Maybe he was; maybe the smoke was his lie because he was lying to himself this whole time, wasn't he? If he wasn't afraid, then why hide the box?

"I'm not afraid," Jack whispered. He turned the lever faster and faster. Round and round. Out sprang Jack. His black lips smiling; his black eyes staring. In the dim light of the room, it looked as though the white dash in the centre of the pupil glistened. Jack slammed the lid down.

With it closed, he felt the pulse beating from the wood onto the palm of his hand. "Not possible," Jack said. "Not bloody possible." He brought the box over to the coffee table and sat on the sofa; dust rose from the fabric and clouded the room. Jack barely noticed it. His eyes stayed fixed on the box. He placed his other hand on top of the box, and there was the pulsing once again. He closed his eyes, felt the coolness of the room, the smell of unuse, and felt the thump thump pulsing through his skin. It was slow and steady. Whatever spirit lived inside the box wasn't experiencing the anxiety that was rippling through Jack.

Jack went to the dresser and grabbed the bottle of wine. He drank. The wine slid down his throat. After a few sips more, Jack dared to return to the sofa. There, still drinking the wine, he stared at the box. When his hand returned to the top of the box, he felt the same steady thump.

"Jesus," Jack said. There was the beginning of a slur in his voice. The part of him that was still sober heard it. In his head, he heard Jackser saying, *oh no, Jesus won't help you kill; only Jack-in-the-Box will do that.* More sips from his wine until he had drunk half the bottle.

"It's not possible," he said. "Not bloody possible."

A wind blew in through the open sitting room door, and it slammed shut. Jack bolted to his feet. Only then did he see on the yellowing wallpaper a picture of Pierce taken in front of the farmhouse fifteen years before. In it, Pierce's hair was still dark, and he was smiling. His eyes were too familiar, too like Jack's own. It was like looking at a version of himself that he would become in another fifteen years.

There was no need to check for a pulse again, as Jack could hear it beating. Jack fled from the room and ran into the kitchen, but he could still hear it. *Thump thump thump*. Jack pressed his hands over his ears and dropped the bottle of wine in the process. The beat drowned out the sound of the crashing glass.

Jack paced the room until the answer came to him and when it did, it was so obvious. There was a drawer in the dresser where Pierce had always kept the odds and ends. Jack opened it and took out the flashlight. He tested it and a brilliant light streamed out, almost blinding him in the process. With lights dancing in his eyes, Jack took the flashlight outside. The light from the flashlight lit the road before him and landed on the tool shed at the back of the house. Jack's late grandfather had been a keen carpenter, as well as a farmer. Twenty years gone now, and all his tools were still in there, rusting away. Jack pulled the lock back on the shed's door and scanned the interior with his torchlight. It illuminated the cobwebs gathering on the lines of unloved tools and the huge iron toolbox. Jack took the shovel nestled between the rake and the scythe and left the shed. There was a plump patch of ground at the back of the house where Jack's granny used to grow vegetables. Jack dug the spade into the earth and began digging the hole. Even out there, with his breathing coming fast and hard from the exertion, he could hear the *thump thump*.

When the hole was three feet deep, Jack walked to the house. With each step he took, the steady *thump thump* grew louder. In the sitting room, Jack picked up the box, but the beating carried through into his skin and grated against his bones. It spread through to his teeth, and he gnashed them together. Jack put the box on the coffee table. He went into the kitchen, retrieved oven mitts from the drawer, and put them on. When he picked up the box again, he could still feel the pulsing through his hands and hear it too, but at least now the pain was tolerable.

He left the farmhouse again. Well into spring now, but the night air was cold, and it slapped him across the face. His footsteps mingled with the *thump thump* inside the box. The torch was tucked away in Jack's armpit. Its light danced across the path, giving flashes of grass. When Jack reached the hole, he dropped the torch onto the ground. Its light skipped the hole, illuminating the grass beyond it. Jack manoeuvred it so that its light reached into the earth. The box continued its beating. Jack held it above the hole. He wanted to drop it straight in there, but the fear of the lid opening and the Jack popping out caused him to drop to his knees and lower the box into the hole.

There, lying on the ground with the stars overhead and the night frost freezing his legs, Jack heard a whisper on the wind. "Jack," the voice said. It was a voice Jack knew well: Pierce's. Only the tone was different— deep, slow, and half-cut with coals.

Jack stood up. "Pierce?" he called. "Pierce? I didn't mean to hurt you. Sure, I didn't think it would work." The wind swirled around Jack once again, but now there was no voice. The only answer, if you could call it one, was the constant beating coming from the hole in the ground.

The shovel was propped against the wall at the back of the house. Jack retrieved it. He scooped dirt from the mound of earth and threw it onto the box. Jack's arm muscles twitched with the next scoop and the next. He continued, only feeling somewhat lighter when he could see the box no more. The Jack of yesterday would have smiled when the hole was filled but the Jack of today couldn't smile. Not when he knew for sure that this box had caused Pierce's death and he had willingly used it. He was a murderer.

It was quiet inside the house. There was the twist and turn of dying logs and the groans of the house as it settled down for the night. Jack paced in the kitchen. The effects of the drink were slowly wearing off and the hangover was kicking in. He could feel the knife blade pushing into his temple and the desert forming inside his mouth. Sipping on water relieved the drought but it did little to help his headache. Jack rubbed his chin, an action he could visualise Pierce doing too, usually when he was staring at Jack with something akin to puzzlement on his face.

When Jack's legs and feet hurt from the constant pacing, he wandered up to bed. While taking off his trousers, he saw the message from Aoife saying that her sister was staying. Jack thought it was just as well for Veronica's crisis; it would've been terrible if Aoife had been there to witness the madness.

Yet maybe she should have been there. It was her fault. She was the one who had wanted to go to that bloody craft fair. If they hadn't gone, none of this mess would've happened. Jack would be guilt-free, and Pierce would be alive, mourning the loss of Mimi or still trying to contact her. Jack was milling it all over when the pulsing started again. It was faint enough at first for Jack to think it was his heart beating. But a quick scan of his pulse and he knew it couldn't be, for his pulse was racing and the thump was still the same slow steady beat. Jack pulled the covers over his head in an attempt to drown it out, but it didn't work.

Jack had never been much of a crier, but he cried there, burying his head underneath the pillow feeling hot wet tears drench the sheets. When the door creaked open, Jack jumped out of bed, hastily dressed, put on his runners, and ran down the stairs. The torch was on the kitchen table, just where Jack had left it. He turned it on and ran around to the side of the house. The mound of earth was undisturbed, even with the force of the vibration that it produced. Wind rattled, the trees shook, and the earth pulsed so much that Jack was sure another hole would open and swallow him.

"I'm sorry, Pierce," Jack screamed. He fell to his knees and pleaded. "I'm fucking sorry." Nothing but the pulsing answered him. Jack's chin dropped to his chest. The farm might be his, but it shouldn't be. He knew that now. Had known as soon as Jackser told him what the Jack-in-the-Box was capable of that he would try it on his uncle and hope for a miracle. Jack went into the house, took his car keys from the table, and drove to the Garda Station. There'd be no lying anymore. He'd need to confess.

They thought he was crazy. Who wouldn't? They had written everything he had said and when the statement had been given, the two guards looked at each other as if to confirm what the other was thinking. One of the guards, a man with a thick red beard and thick red hair, exited the room, and Jack was left alone with the other guard, a woman with a blonde bob that reminded Jack of the 90s.

"You doing okay, Jack?" she had asked. "Want me to

give your wife a call?"

"No, don't ring her," Jack had said. "You'll only have her worrying."

The woman with the 90s-style bob smiled, and that was the end of the conversation. Ten minutes later, the red-haired Garda came back. The two of them glanced at each other again. Jack knew by that glance that they must have had a little something going on because it was the same way Aoife used to look at Jack at the start of their marriage when they were co-conspirators.

"We'd like you to talk with someone," the red-haired Garda said. "He's not available to talk now but he's going to be in contact with you later today. We know you're raring to get to the farm for the milking, but we're going to have to go with you. Just to make sure you're okay until you see the doctor."

"To see if I'm crazy?" Jack asked.

"He'll be able to talk to you at ten. Eleven at the latest. You'll hardly notice that we're there."

Jack nodded, for he knew there was nothing he could say to stop them. They wouldn't let him drive his car, so he had to sit in the backseat of the Garda car and answer their polite, meaningless questions. When he refused to laugh at their unfunny jokes, they eventually gave up the small talk and let Jack stew. He needed the quiet as they approached the farm. He couldn't bear having to talk to them and deal with the pulsing, but when they arrived at the farm, everything was quiet. Not even a slight beat.

Jack walked to the back of the house. The mound of earth was still there, as was the shovel, propped up against the wall. The two guards had followed Jack and were watching him with their heads tilted to the side.

"When my father died, I'd awful guilt," the red-haired Garda said. "I used to blame myself for it for years in the way you're doing."

Jack inhaled the morning air. With it still and the morning golden, it was easy to believe that he had just been blaming himself. Not to mention that he had been drinking too. Not just drinking but mixing his drinks, which was something Jack never did. "I suppose it was signing the papers that must've triggered something in my head," Jack said. "I was talking like a madman, wasn't I?" Jack laughed. Out here in the light, it was easy to believe it had been a hallucination. "Well, I better get on with this milking." He walked away from the guards; he knew they were following him. Let them follow. "Will I make ye a cup of tea before I start? I wouldn't mind one myself."

"We're okay, Jack," the blonde guard said.

"Grand," Jack said. He went into the kitchen, made himself a flask of tea, and ate one of the breakfast bars that Aoife had left in the press.

With tea in hand, he went to the milking parlour and began his morning's work. When he was almost finished, he heard Aoife's voice outside. Jack peeped out of the parlour and saw the two guards talking to her. Whatever she said had them laughing.

The red-haired guard walked over to Jack. "We're going to head off away now, Jack. Aoife said she'll stay with you. The doctor's going to be here with you in an hour. Is that okay with you?"

"You told Aoife what happened?" Jack asked. He rubbed his chin and once again could imagine Pierce doing the same action. Before the guard had a chance to respond, Jack said, "Well, I suppose she needed to know."

Aoife strolled over. She mustn't have been at work because she was wearing a pink tracksuit that she only wore when she was going off on long walks. "How's the milking going?" she asked.

"All good," Jack said. "I'm almost finished."

"Will I make you a cup of tea?" Aoife asked.

"I'd love tea," Jack said.

The guards said goodbye. Jack watched them drive away before returning to the cows. When he had finished the milking, he went into the kitchen. Aoife had her back turned to him and was pouring water from the kettle into two mugs. "I'll put an extra spoon of sugar into your tea; you'll need it after the night you had."

"Thanks," Jack said. He sat down and watched her take the teabags out of the mug and add a splash of milk into each one. "You heard about what happened then."

Aoife brought the mugs to the table and placed a white cup in front of Jack. "I did. You must be wrecked now."

Jack yawned. "I'll probably go for a lie down after this. Or after the doctor comes to see me anyway. For all I know, he'll put me in the mental and I'll have my fill of sleep." Jack took a sip of the tea. It was hot and sweet, and he was delighted with the extra spoonful of sugar. "It's a different brand of tea, is it?"

"It is," Aoife said. "It's all organic ingredients, so I've been told."

"It's not bad for one of your fancy teas. Normally, I can't stand them." Jack drank. It tasted even better on the second drink. He yawned again and rubbed his eyes. "Jesus, the tiredness is catching up with me. I can't remember the last time I did an all-nighter."

"Would you like a biscuit?" Aoife asked softly. "I bought you some custard creams." She retrieved them from the worktop without waiting for Jack's response. She opened the packet and left it on the table.

Jack took one and dipped it into the tea. "You're too good to be getting me fancy tea and biscuits. I thought you were going to be eating the ear off me for making a show of myself."

"Why would I do that?" Aoife asked, puzzled.

Jack took another biscuit from the packet and gobbled it down with a mouthful of tea. "Did the guards tell you what I thought happened?"

"About the Jack-in-the-Box and you thinking it had caused Pierce's death? They told me everything."

Jack felt a tingling in his arms and a slight ringing in his ears. An effect of no sleep, he thought, and he drank more of his tea. "And you think I'm mad." He sighed. "I think I'm mad too if it makes any difference."

"I don't think you're mad," Aoife said. "The guards do. They didn't want to let me on my own with you, but I told them I'd be grand."

The tingling spread onto Jack's chest. He rubbed it as he digested what Aoife said. "Why is it you don't think I'm mad? Because you already knew I was mad?" He attempted to laugh, but it was difficult with the tingling spreading to his throat.

"The Sunday after we went to the market, I went back. Remember that Sunday you were busy here with the farm doing your list of everything you wanted to do?"

Jack nodded.

"I met a strange man there, and he told me a very strange story about selling you a Jack-in-the-Box. He told me all sorts of things, Jack. He knew all sorts of things about me and you. He even knew about Toby and myself."

Jack's throat wasn't tingling now; it was numb. His face was numb, and when he tried to speak, his tongue just lolled from the side of his mouth.

"Can you not speak, Jack?" Aoife asked. She brought her mug to her mouth and smiled over her cup. "You were right about Toby. So was Jackser. He's an odd man,

Jackser, isn't he? I thought he was crazy, but I still bought this from him." Aoife stood up and retrieved a black box from her pink handbag. She placed it on the kitchen table. Jack's eyes, painful to move, stared at the skull on its centre and the silver writing above the skull that said Death Tea. "He even knew that you had hidden the Jack-in-the-Box in the dresser. Seeing it there made me believe him. Then when I heard about your confession to the guards, I said feck it, I might as well take the chance with the tea. Jackser said the tea would kill the drinker within twenty minutes. He said it'll look natural, too. I hope he's right, Jack. I truly do."

Aoife checked the time on her phone. "You know the best part of all this, Jack, is that even if it doesn't work, no one will believe a word you say. You're the mad fella. But it does look like it's working. Sure, look at the cut of you. You can't even move, can you?"

Jack's eyes blurred. His heart was wild inside his chest until slowly, slowly it eased, and his eyes closed. He could hear Aoife humming "Pop Goes the Weasel" until sound faded, and then there was nothing.

The End

ACKNOWLEDGEMENTS

Thank you to everyone who read these stories and helped make them better. And thank you for reading my book.

ABOUT THE AUTHOR

J.M Clerkin lives in the southeast of Ireland. When she is not reading or writing, you can find her exploring Ireland and beyond.